HIGHLAND ENCHANTMENT

Highland Heartstrings, Book 2

by

Brenna Ash

ARE YOU SIGNED UP FOR DRAGONBLADE'S BLOG?

You'll get the latest news and information on exclusive giveaways, exclusive excerpts, coming releases, sales, free books, cover reveals and more.

Check out our complete list of authors, too!

No spam, no junk. That's a promise!

Sign Up Here

www.dragonbladepublishing.com

Dearest Reader;

Thank you for your support of a small press. At Dragonblade Publishing, we strive to bring you the highest quality Historical Romance from some of the best authors in the business. Without your support, there is no 'us', so we sincerely hope you adore these stories and find some new favorite authors along the way.

Happy Reading!

CEO, Dragonblade Publishing

Additional Dragonblade books by Author Brenna Ash

Highland Heartstrings Series
Highland Treasure (Book 1)
Highland Enchantment (Book 2)

Rogues of Redemption Series
Sweet Rogue O' Mine (Book 1)
Rogue You Like a Hurricane (Book 2)
No Rogue Like You (Book 3)
Nobody's Rogue (Book 4)
Here I Rogue Again (Book 5)

The Lyon's Den Series
The Lyon's Last Gamble

CHAPTER ONE

Scottish Highlands
Summer

RORY HART GRUNTED as he swung his arm up and his fingers found a small slip of ledge to slide into. He pushed off with his booted foot and repeated the gesture. Below him, swift waves crashed onto rocks, breaking up the bright white peaks. The briny smell of the sea surrounded him and he inhaled deeply as he made his way up the wall of rock.

He could spend all of his days for the rest of his life out here doing this same thing every day and he would die a very happy man. There was no one to bother him. No one nagging him about responsibility or what he should be doing for the family. For the clan.

Being the second born son of the laird, he didn't have the amount of responsibility that had been placed on his older brother, Alpin's, shoulders since birth, but he had his share.

And he'd rather ignore them.

There was naught he disliked more than being holed up in Hartsmoor Castle. His familial home was massive and held a commanding presence in their part of the highlands, but whenever he was indoors, he longed to be outside. He felt held down. Closed in. A prisoner of sorts.

Reaching the top of the rock, he pulled himself up and over the edge to the summit. He rolled his burning shoulders in an attempt to ease the tightness from the effort of the climb. He looked at his fingers, the knuckles bloody where he'd managed to scrape the skin off when he dragged them across the rough stone surface.

But sore and bloody, he didn't care. Nay, the beautiful view laid out afore him was worth every scrape of skin. Every sore muscle. He dropped to the ground and brought a knee up to rest his arm upon as he lifted his chin and squinted at the sun.

The silence of his rowdy siblings and castle life was a welcome reprieve. There were plenty of noises here to fill his ears. The sound of the crashing waves. The birds sing-song. The faint rustle of the wind blowing through the grass and trees, shifting the leaves.

All of them were amongst his favorite sounds. Natural sounds that he expected to hear when he was in the midst of nature.

Here he didn't have to listen to his mother, Lillias, lovely as she was, lecture him about taking unnecessary risks.

"Ye will fall one day. Yer fingers or boots will slip and down ye will go." She would make an exaggerated sweep of her arm, arcing it through the air. "And we will ne'er ken. For days ye could lay upon the rocks, a bloody mess, or worse, dead, and we willnae ken. 'Tis too dangerous." Then she would drop a kiss on his cheek afore patting his head as if he were a wee lad and move on to trying to convince his father, Arthur, laird of clan Hart, to order him to stop.

But his father kenned better. The highlands called to Rory. The fresh air beckoned him.

His family would never be able to drag him away from them.

He refused to be remanded inside doing Lord kens what.

Leaning back on his palms, he let the early summer sun warm his face and skin. He closed his eyes and took a slow, cleansing breath.

Soon, no matter how much he didn't want to, Rory would need to return to Hartsmoor. Back to the raucous that was his family. Having four siblings meant that the castle they called home was never quiet—especially with three sisters.

Here, though, in the highlands, in the trees, scaling rocky cliffs and hiking mountains, Rory felt like he could forget the rest of the world existed. It was just him and nature. No pressure. No demands.

He could just be.

Sighing, he pushed himself up off the ground and dusted the backside of his trews off. He began his descent, choosing a different path than the way he had come up. As he made his way down, he saw a hawk circling in the distance.

Something in the area must have perished, or it was tracking its prey. Either way, Rory was sure it would not be long afore it dove down and snatched whatever creature it was that the bird had spotted.

The closer he got to Hartsmoor the more solemn his mood grew. His shoulders felt heavier. His feet moved a little slower. That always happened when he spent a day doing what he loved only to return to the confines of his family home.

Rory loved his family. Every single sibling. His parents. He never wished ill will to fall upon any of them and would not cope well with one of them becoming injured. Was it wrong then, that even though he loved them, he didn't want to be around them?

His sister, Moira, had an independent streak that their parents had tried to break her of. All the good that did. Instead, she deceived them all by concocting a plan to visit her best friend for an extended period of time and traveled the highlands with a MacLeod. Not just any MacLeod, but Laird MacLeod's first-born son. The clan was Hart's sworn enemy at the time. Had been for years long afore Rory's father had been born.

Now, they were married, uniting the clans and bringing to light a history that none of them had been aware of.

When their father had found out what she had done, Rory thought he was going to meet an early grave. Arthur was ready to scorch the earth from their lands to the MacLeods.

But it all worked out in the end and now she and her husband, Errol, were building a new life together on a parcel of land that now acted as a bridge of peace betwixt the Hart and the MacLeod clans. With Moira and Errol's settlement there, the lands were joined, creating a new future devoid of the fighting that had long defined their families.

Walking up the road that would lead him to Hartsmoor, Rory dragged his feet with each step. For some reason, he felt unsettled. As if bad news was headed his way. He paused and sucked in a huge gulp of crisp highland air, letting it slowly out through his nose as he gazed at the trees lining either side of the road. If he turned left the road would take him to the bustling village where merchants of all kinds were selling their wares—jewelry, embroidery, clothing. Aught that one could imagine would be sold on the streets. Then there was the baker, with his tasty treats and breads. The ale maker with his honey and heather mead. The blacksmith—one of the finest this side of the high-lands. Rory himself had purchased a small dagger from him on one of his trips into the village. It was made of supreme crafts-manship.

Entering the bailey, a young page ran up to him. "Master Rory, yer father awaits yer return. He wishes to speak to ye immediately."

Rory furrowed his brow. "Did he say why?" He questioned.

The lad shook his head. "Nay, only that ye were to see him as soon as ye were back. He doesnae wish ye to do aught else."

Rory cleared his throat and pushed his hands through his hair. What could his father possibly want now? Unless his mother had talked Arthur into trying to dissuade him from his mountain and rock climbing. It wouldn't be the first time, and he was for certs that it would not be the last time either. But the page spoke with an undertone of urgency, so Rory doubted his required presence was due to his activities.

In the Great Hall, his father stood, tall and strong, fiery red hair crowning his head with a bushy beard to match. His barrel arms were crossed as he spoke.

"I thought it best I meet ye at the door to ensure that ye actually come and meet me." His words weren't harsh. They held a hint of mirth behind them and when he smiled, Rory kenned that the subject of the time he spent outside and away from Hartsmoor wasn't going to be the topic of conversation.

"Let us go to my study." He looked around, as if searching for someone, and appearing to be happy that whoever it was, wasn't about, he asked, "How was yer climb today?"

Rory felt the tension ease a bit from his shoulders. "'Twas a good day," he answered, stretching his neck from side to side.

He followed his father into his study and shut the door behind them when Arthur waved his hand for him to do so.

"I am glad ye had a pleasant climb." Arthur sat down at his massive desk, piled high with ledgers and account books. "I must say I am happy that ye returned earlier than usual. I need ye to go to the village."

Rory frowned. "What for?"

Arthur tapped his index finger on the desk for a few long moments. If Rory didn't ken him any better, he would think that he was contemplating what he was going to say. But that wouldn't be the Arthur he kenned. Nay, the Arthur he kenned always kenned what to say. No matter the situation, Arthur was always there with the right words.

Arthur formed a fist and rested it gently on the desktop. "There has been an accident—"

Rory pushed out of the chair he had been sitting in and straightened. "Is it ma? Alpin? Eilidh or Morven?" Nay, if it were a Hart family member, his father would have gone himself and not waited for Rory to return. Though a messenger would have been waiting for him when he arrived to send him to meet them.

"Or is it Moira? Did that MacLeod bastard hurt Moira? I will kill him," Rory threatened as he clenched his fists.

His father raised an eyebrow and motioned for him to sit back down.

"Nay, the family is fine. Though I would advise ye to choose yer words wisely when speaking of Laird MacLeod. He is now yer brother-in-law."

Rory dropped back into the chair, his anger ebbing at the relief of learning his sister fared well. He still held lingering doubts about her new husband, even if his sister seemed blissfully happy in her new marriage.

"There was a carriage accident outside of the village. A woman, she is a wee bit bruised, but otherwise unharmed when her carriage overturned."

Rory shrugged, unable to understand why that was any of his concern. Carriages overturned on a nearly daily basis. He had never been called upon for one afore.

"She is demanding help to be transported to her betrothed, which is where she was traveling to when the accident occurred."

"Demanding transport?" Rory did not like where this conversation was headed. Anyone demanding aught of the Harts was clearly someone of higher standing. No one else would dare to make such a demand. Irritation filled him. He could not stand nobles and the entitlement they seemed to carry around with them like a shield wherever they went. Dealing with them was a nightmare. "'Tis quite forward of them, dinnae ye think?"

Arthur sighed heavily. "This is something ye must do."

Rory shook his head. "Nay. I willnae."

"I am demanding that ye escort her. 'Tis no' up for debate. Ye will heed my command, son."

Straightening in the chair, Rory studied his father's face. In all his years he couldn't remember a time when his father gave him a direct order such as this.

"Why cannae one of our warrior's assist the woman? We have plenty. For certs we could spare one or two to play watcher of this woman who feels so entitled that she can make demands of clan Hart. *Of Laird Hart.*"

"She may be entitled. Hell, she may be a thorn in yer side for the length of yer travels, howe'er, her family has connections. Weel tied connections that could serve us weel. Providing assistance will show goodwill and that can go a long way for us in the future. Ye ne'er ken when we may need to call upon them."

Rory rolled his eyes. "Is she a lady, then?"

"No' yet. But she is betrothed to the MacDonell son."

Rory groaned. His father needed not say aught further. The MacDonell clan held lands in the north close to Hart lands and undertaking such an endeavor would indeed bode well for their future.

"Shite." Rory grunted.

"I need Alpin here, but e'en if I didnae, he doesnae possess yer skills. He doesnae ken e'ery inch of the terrain as ye do. It must be ye."

Chewing the inside of his cheek to stop him from saying things he would regret, Rory pushed up from the chair. Anger would get him nowhere. And he couldn't show his reluctance to his clan. Such disrespect to their laird would not be withstood.

"A sennight. I will agree to that. Just until I can get her to safety and then I will send her on her way and return home."

His father nodded. "She is currently in the village waiting."

"Weel, then," Rory clapped his hands and rubbed them together. "I best no' keep her waiting," he finished sarcastically.

Arthur frowned. "Mayhap ye should clean up and change afore ye go."

Rory shook his head, his jaw clenched as he looked down at his dusty clothes. "Nay. I will go now." He exited his father's study, annoyance hanging over him like a heavy woolen cloak wet from a day's rain. Making his way to the stables to ready his horse, he brushed the dust and dirt from his clothes. He laughed unbelievably. His father wanted him to change. What for? So he could just get dirty again on his way to meet the woman and the ride back? Absolutely not.

By the time his horse was ready, irritation filled his veins as he thought of how quickly he could get her to safety so he could return to Hartsmoor.

CHAPTER TWO

ALANA DURAN LET out a frustrated growl as she circled the muddy wreckage of her overturned carriage, throwing her hands up in defeat. The two guards that had been escorting her were nowhere to be found.

She was alone.

In the woods.

Far away from her home.

Her father would be furious. When only two men arrived at their home days ago to take her to her betrothed—something she still could not fathom—he had insisted that she deserved more protection than what was originally offered. They had to wait another fortnight for reinforcements to arrive. As soon as they were far enough away from Auchenford Castle, her now former home, those very same guards that had presented themselves as additional help to escort Alana to her new home, left them alone once again, so it was only the three of them.

Alana couldn't ascertain if it was because her husband-to-be was uncaring for her welfare or unable to finance such an escort. Neither option set her mind at ease.

The weather had turned from pleasant enough to a full-on drenching rain not long afore they crashed. As the carriage rolled over, she found herself being tossed about, rolling along with it, trying to find something stable to hang onto so she wouldn't be thrown from the cabin. As the carriage came to a rest with a severe jolt, upside down on the soft, wet ground, Alana had taken a steadying breath, thankful that the carriage hadn't come crashing down upon her body.

She was sore and was for certs that in the next day or two her body would be dotted with numerous bruises, but she was alive and that was what was most important.

That is what her betrothed would be happy to hear about. Wouldn't he? She asked herself. Actually, she was unsure of the answer he would give. She had never met the man. His age, his demeanor, his looks—all were a mystery to her.

The only thing she kenned was that her father and he had come to an agreement and in doing so, she was to be sent northeast to be married. She would be lady of the keep or castle. She laughed bitterly. She didn't even ken what the name of her betrothed's residence was.

Her boots were soaked through, making her feet cold even though it was early summer. Up here, the weather was cooler than it was at her home in the lowlands near the English border. A wet chill hung in the air now that the rain had subsided and the fact that the surrounding trees were packed so closely together that nary a ray of the faint sun could filter through—when the sun decided to reappear. A fire to warm her cold toes near sounded like heaven to her right now.

The betrothal ring her future husband had given her via a proxy was still nestled on her finger, a stark reminder of what her goal was—to marry. She would need to find transport to the place she would soon call home. It was what her father expected of her, and she would not let him down. She wouldn't be the one to bring disrespect to their family by not following through with the order she had been tasked with.

Looking down, she noted the sad state of her gown. It had been perfect when she had left Auchenford Castle, but now not only was it wet and dirty, with clumps of mud stuck to it, a large tear rented the center of the skirt. She would mend it after it had been properly laundered, but until then she would change into another gown packed in the trunks that had been secured to the carriage afore they set out on their journey.

Her trunks!

Searching the surrounding area, she found them both and whispered a quick prayer that, even though they had broken away from the carriage, the lids remained locked in place. At least she wouldn't have to launder all the items that she had brought.

"Hello?" She called out, foolishly hoping that her escorts had just wandered into the woods to relieve themselves.

She waited a few moments.

Naught.

No answer. No shuffling of someone walking through the woods.

Sinking down onto a weathered tree stump, worn smooth over time, she thought of her current predicament. What was she to do now? She had no idea of what direction they were going other than northeast. Her father hadn't told her much. Only that she needed to marry and he had found her a husband. The union would bring much needed coin to their depleted coffers. Her father hadn't mentioned the sad state of their financial situation, but she had heard enough conversations betwixt he and others to learn that Auchenford Castle would not remain in Duran hands much longer if they could not find the needed funding to maintain it.

Understanding that was why she hadn't questioned or pushed back to her father once he had told her of his plans. Not that she could have anyway. She was his daughter and she wasn't naive enough not to realize a young woman's place in the world. She was there as a bartering tool. Naught more. When she'd first learned of her place and function as a young lass, she had been upset. Her mother had explained that it was just the way things were. She, too, had been bartered by her father when she was young in exchange for land and coin.

And now Alana saw that this deal struck betwixt her father

and her husband-to-be was the same thing.

She only hoped that the man she was to marry was close to her age and pleasant to gaze upon. That he would be a kind husband and a good father to the children that he would no doubt insist she bear him. That last piece was to be expected. Every laird needed an heir.

And for that, she would also do her duty.

It would just be much easier to perform said duty if her future husband wasn't an old crotchet.

Alana took solace in kenning that even though her parent's marriage had been arranged, they enjoyed a happy union and a life filled with love.

Footsteps stomping the ground nearby pulled Alana from her thoughts and she stood quickly, trying to quickly brush the mud, dirt, and leaves from her skirts. A quick flash of worry washed over her but quickly diminished as three young lads appeared, stopping short when they noticed her and her overturned carriage.

"Are ye weel, my lady?" The tallest boy of the group asked, stepping forward, concern creasing his forehead.

She nodded. "Aye, I am. Thank ye. I am in need of assistance though." She waved her hand toward the carriage as if they hadn't seen it.

He looked from her to the carriage and back again, nodding. "We can bring ye back to the village with us. 'Tis just a short walk."

"Thank ye. But what of my things?"

"Men will come to retrieve those and bring them to ye in the village."

"I cannae stay at the village. I need to get to my betrothed."

The boy scratched his chin and shrugged. "That is no' for me to say." He turned on his heel and began walking back the same way he had come from.

Was he going to leave her there? For certs not. "Wait," she called out.

The lad paused and threw her a look over his shoulder. "The village is this way." He pointed in front of him.

Sighing, she kenned she wouldn't get any more information from him. She took a deep breath, swallowing her frustration as she quickly made her way to his side.

The other two lads had already run ahead. Probably to warn the village that an outsider was coming.

"Did ye perchance see two men on yer way here?"

The boy shook his head. "Nay. No one. Why do ye ask?"

She blew out a breath. "I was just trying to locate my guards."

"I havenae seen anyone. Were they hurt in the accident?"

"Nay. I checked the surrounding area. 'Tis only me here."

"Sorry, my lady. I am of no assistance for that."

"'Tis fine. Mayhap they made their way to yer village afore ye began yer journey here," she said wistfully. "'Tis possible I will see them there."

His look told her that he didn't believe her, and quite frankly, she didn't believe it herself. But she couldn't fathom why they would have abandoned her. There would for certs be a consequence to pay for such an act. How could she explain to the villagers that her guards had left her without nary a care for her well-being? It was embarrassing. What if they thought she was a horrible person and that the men escaped the first chance they got?

She sighed as she continued to walk beside the lad. She was not dastardly. And she was not some miscreant off the street. Surely, her trunks alone would prove that.

If she wasn't so dirty and her dress in such a state, they would easily be able to tell. But not in her current condition. They might even think she was lying about the contents of what her trunks contained.

As they neared the village, she clenched her hands into fists. Damn those guards. Every single last one of them. The two that had run, and all the others that left the moment they were out of view of Auchenford. She would ensure her father kenned about what had happened.

She bit the inside of her cheek. She no longer fell under her father's responsibility. That now fell to her betrothed.

Fine, then. She would ensure that her husband-to-be kenned of her abandonment.

They crested a hill and the village appeared on the other side, bustling with life. A small crowd had gathered waiting for them to arrive. The two lads that had run ahead must have made everyone aware of her appearance.

Refusing to be looked down upon, she straightened her shoulders and lifted her chin, taking confident steps forward as she entered the village.

"Welcome to Dornichton, my lady." A woman that appeared to be around the same age as her mother stepped forward and greeted her.

"Thank ye." Alana looked around at the people gathered, feeling like she was a prized hog on display. "I need to secure transport to my betrothed. Have ye seen my two guards come through? They were escorting me when the accident occurred."

"I am Tilly. Nay, I am sorry, but I havenae seen anyone from away come through the village. We would ken, as all of us are local." She assessed Alana's gown. "Outsiders tend to stick out like sore thumbs, if ye ken what my meaning."

Irritation bubbled at the realization that her guards had truly abandoned her. Did no one in her soon-to-be husband's clan have any integrity? From what she had seen so far, she would say not. Dread settled deep in her belly at the thought that entered her mind. What type of life was she destined to live once she arrived at her new home? None of it seemed appealing from what she'd seen of his men.

Her father's guards would never have done such a thing. And in the off chance someone did, her father would have had them punished severely. The men would have been whipped and then spent a night or two in the dungeon with just water and bread to eat.

Alana could only hope that her husband would treat such desertion of duty in much the same way.

"Word has been sent to Laird Hart. He will ensure ye are taken care of."

Alana sighed. "When will he arrive? I really must be going on my way. We had a schedule to adhere to."

Tilly's mouth turned down. "Again, my lady, I apologize. I have no control o'er our laird and his timeframes. Howe'er we have sent for him and he or a delegate will arrive to assist ye."

She wasn't happy with that answer, but she also couldn't blame the villagers. They were only doing what they would normally do when a stranger arrived in their village.

Tilly smiled. "Come. Let us get some food in yer belly whilst ye wait. Ye must be starving."

As if on cue, Alana's stomach let out a loud grumble and Tilly grinned.

"Aye, as I said, ye must be starving after yer journey."

She let the woman lead her down the street and to a quaint cottage. Ushering Alana inside, she urged her to take a seat at one of the empty tables.

The smells of fresh baked bread and roasted meat filled her senses.

Two hours later, Alana's appetite was sated and she warmed herself by the hearth, a warm mug of cider in her hands. Her boots sat near the flame, drying, along with her soaked stockings, which were hanging from nearby hooks.

Murmurs from those around her caught her attention and she looked over to the doorway and her breath caught in her throat.

A fierce Highlander had entered, and people approached him, bowing in greeting.

W-w-was he to be her escort? He looked terrifying and she fought against the shiver that traveled up her spine.

He was tall, easily over a foot taller than she, with light brown hair and piercing green eyes. A thick beard covered his strong jaw, a deep scar splitting his left cheek in two, and he appeared unkempt. Dust and dirt covered his clothing.

Was this Laird Hart? He was younger than she expected him to be. Furthermore, he obviously had no self-respect in that he had not even bothered to wash himself up to greet a guest.

She almost laughed. Probably would have if she hadn't been caught by his intense gaze as if a gnat in a web, unable to get away. She kenned she was judging him unfairly considering her appearance was no better than his. At least all of his clothes were free of tears. She could not say the same of hers.

Setting the cider down, Alana stood and approached the man. From this close, he looked even bigger than she had originally thought. He remained silent, looking unimpressed as he assessed her.

"Laird Hart," she called, dipping into a curtsy to show her respect.

"Is my father."

"Pardon?"

He sighed, irritation lacing his voice. "Laird Hart is my father. I am Rory Hart, one of his sons."

She pressed her lips together. His brooding presence intimidated her. But she couldn't let that stop her. She needed to push forward.

With a defiant lift of her chin, something that she hoped would show him that she would not back down, she said, "I need transport and lodging. I am due to my betrothed in the coming days."

Laughing loudly, he crossed his arms, his dark green eyes traveling from her face and lower, resting on her bosom afore moving lower, then sweeping back up to meet her gaze. "I suggest ye walk."

"Excuse me? Do ye ken who I am? I am Laird Duran's daughter. His only daughter. Ye are required to get me safely to my destination."

He lifted a brow and narrowed his eyes.

"I believe ye have mistaken me for someone else. I dinnae

take orders from a lass." He spun and walked toward the door.

"Wait!" Alana called after him, following quickly. She picked up her skirts so that she could move faster. Then, remembering her boots and stockings, she ran back to the fire to retrieve them, afore running back toward the door. "Sir, wait, please," she begged.

His back stiffened, but he paused. They were outside now and had caught the attention of many of the villagers.

"Ye cannae dismiss me. Werenae ye sent to assist me in my travels?"

He clucked his tongue as he turned and pierced her with a non-plussed look that had her taking a step back. Had she pushed him too far?

"I was." He stepped closer, bending down so he could look her in the eye. "Howe'er I dinnae take kindly to being ordered about by a lass. Especially one I have only had the unfortunate circumstance to just meet."

She chewed her lip as she began to wring her hands together. She could see how he could be affronted by that.

He looked down at her bare feet and the boots and stockings she'd set on the ground, a frown turning down the corners of his mouth.

She huffed in a breath. "I do apologize. 'Tis been a trying day. My guards have abandoned me—"

"I am beginning to see why," he interjected.

Taking a steadying breath, Alana wet her lips, but ignored his jab. She was aware of the villagers watching them with smiles upon their faces. Some of them giggling as they saw the scene unfolding betwixt them, clearly amused by their exchange. Her cheeks heated with embarrassment.

"As I was saying," she continued. "I need yer help. Am I correct to assume that yer father, Laird Hart, sent ye here for that?" She waited silently, wanting to shrink into the ground under his scrutiny as he studied her.

"Aye," he finally agreed, and she let out the breath she had been holding.

She nodded, trying to think of the words that wouldn't upset him. Though she didn't ken what to say, since the man standing afore her looked to be easily angered.

The villagers still watched them and her face burned with humiliation. He was to be her escort and the sooner they began their journey, the sooner it would be done and over with and she could forget this whole exchange.

It was something that she would never speak of again. She just needed to get to her husband-to-be.

And then she could forget Rory Hart existed.

$$\text{\textbf{---◆}\relbar\relbar\relbar\relbar\relbar\relbar\relbar\textbf{◆---}}$$

CHAPTER THREE

T HE NEXT FEW days would prove to be miserable. Rory could predict that without any doubt. The lass was already a thorn in his side, even if she was more than pleasant to his eyes.

He picked up one of the travel sacks he had brought with him and just as he went to hand it to Alana, she jumped up and down excitedly, clapping her hands together. Lord help him.

"My trunks!" She pushed past him with more strength than he thought she harbored and unclasped the hinge before swinging the lid open. "Finally, I can change into dry clothes that arenae caked with mud and torn to shreds."

Rory dropped his chin to his chest and sighed, summoning his patience. "If ye plan to change, be quick aboot it. We leave shortly," he said gruffly.

Alana gave him a droll look, but snatched a few items from the chest, and hurried to find Tilly so the young woman could point her to a private place where she could change and dress in clean clothes.

Tilly would help the lass, he was for certs. Always one to please, she would offer to assist afore Alana even thought of asking.

Walking to her trunk he inspected the items inside. There was no way they were bringing all of these items along with them. She would need to choose a few essential pieces to pack and then they would be on their way.

After what had seemed too much time had passed, Alana reappeared, dressed in a blue gown made of a rich material that showed her status and station, reminding him that she was soon to be a lady. She was a laird's daughter. One that, apparently, stayed cloistered indoors considering the gown she now donned. It was much too nice for hiking, but he had a feeling she wouldn't take too kindly to him pointing that out. At least clean, dry boots covered her feet—a practical choice—and her face had been washed of the streaks of dirt that were there when Rory had first seen her.

He quickly stepped away from the trunk, not wanting her to think he had been rifling through her things. Instead, he held out the empty travel sack he had tried to offer her earlier.

Her eyes fell to his hands and then back to his gaze, her brows crinkling. "What is that?"

"What does it look like? 'Tis a bag for ye to put yer items in." He urged her to take it, but she shook her head.

"I have my trunks already filled with my things. I dinnae need a sack," her voice dripped with disgust.

"Yer trunks will be delivered to yer destination, but no' by us. We move on foot. We cannae carry yer trunks."

Her pretty mouth opened in shock. "On foot? What are ye saying?"

Rory inhaled a long breath. "We are only taking the essentials since we are carrying our things. We are walking. I suggest ye pack what ye need." He turned on his heel, but paused and spun around. "And only what ye need," he added firmly.

Alana crossed her arms stubbornly. "I willnae leave my things behind. Ye are jesting."

He leveled his gaze on Alana, clashing with her hazel eyes. "I am most certainly no'. And ye arenae leaving them behind. They will be delivered to yer new home."

"Ye cannae expect me to walk. I was being transported in a carriage. I expect the same," she said with a huff, her voice loud.

Shrill, and getting higher with each word she spoke.

Once again, Rory cursed his father for sending him on this foolhardy mission.

"Weel, my lady," he said sarcastically. "I am neither yer father nor yer betrothed. I dinnae travel by carriage. I was on my way to a days' long hike when I got tasked with escorting ye to where ye need to be. And hiking I will be doing."

Her eyes widened, but she remained silent.

"Now, we leave soon. Leave most of what ye have packed in yer trunks and only bring what ye absolutely need." He planted his feet and crossed his arms, leaving no room for argument, and waited for her to do as she was told.

Alana huffed as she looked from her trunks to the bag he had dropped at her feet when she refused to take it. "I have ne'er been treated with such disrespect," she snapped as she snatched up the sack. "My future husband will hear of this treatment. He willnae be happy. Ye will see. I will ensure that ye pay," she threatened, moving to one of the trunks and began to stuff things inside, mumbling the whole time.

Rory rolled his eyes as he watched her choose items that would be of little use on their journey. "Ye neednae aught fancy. We will be hiking through the Highlands, no' attending ceremonies and *ceilidhs*." In his own pack, he had all the essentials they would need. He thought about what the coming night would hold. If she was this upset about their travels, he could only imagine what her reaction would be when they made camp later this eve.

Her shrill cries and constant complaints would for certs scare away any wee beasties hiding in the trees. They needn't fear an attack from any wild creatures. The beasts would stay far away from them.

"What exactly do ye propose that I bring then? Unlike ye, I am obviously no' accustomed to traipsing through the woods to get to my destination."

He fought a smile. He didn't want her to ken her reaction

amused him.

Tilly appeared with a bundle of food that she handed him, and he found space in his pack to add it.

"Thank ye. Ye are much too kind."

"Och," Tilly swept the air with her hand in dismissal. "I cannae have the laird's son starving now can I?"

"Starving would be an improvement," Alana mumbled.

"What was that, Lass?" Rory asked, once again amused.

"Stop calling me lass," she snapped. "I have a name. Ye can call me Lady Alana or Miss Duran. Either would be acceptable but stop calling me lass."

"Are ye ready, Lady Alana?" He drawled.

She looked at her trunk and then at her pack and shrugged. "I suppose. I have no idea. Yer instructions were truly lacking. Much like yer manners."

Tilly gasped in surprise.

Rory chuckled. He couldn't help it.

"Let us go. We've much road to cover afore we can rest for the night."

Once they were outside of the village, Rory set a brisk pace, not looking back to see if she was keeping up. A spike of guilt slithered up his spine. If his father saw how he was behaving, he would box his ears at the very least. But that was Arthur's own fault for forcing this damned task upon him. He had been perfectly happy earlier. Ready to prepare for another hike that would take him away from Hartsmoor for a few days, a sennight even. His favorite thing to do—to be alone.

One could argue he was indeed being taken away from home for a few days, but it wasn't the same. He wasn't alone. He wasn't able to hear the beauty of the environ surrounding him. Nay, instead all he heard was her unhappy mumbling behind him, like a constant chatter drowning out any peace and quiet he would normally glean as he hiked.

He fully expected her to fall behind due to the pace he was keeping. He kenned he was being an arse. Kenned full well. So, he was surprised when he turned to look over his shoulder and found her right behind him.

Even more surprised to find her complaining had ceased. The look of irritation she had worn earlier had been replaced by determination. Her face was red with exertion.

A sense of pride warmed him, but he quickly tamped it down. Why the hell should he feel pride that she was determined to keep up—even if he had purposely set a fast pace kenning she would have difficulty with it.

He slowed as they came to a bubbling burn. Alana slowed as well, her chest heaving from the struggle of walking so quickly, and again, he felt a wee surge of guilt.

"We need to cross. 'Tis narrower here so 'twill be easier." He stepped into the water, and turned to her, offering his hand.

Refusing, she let out an exasperated breath as she stubbornly hitched up her skirts and began to cross. Only for her boot to slip on a wet stone causing her to splash into the water, an oath passing her lips.

He didn't catch her. Again, he was acting like an arse.

Which only angered her even further. Dripping wet, her hair clinging to her cheeks, she stomped out of the burn, dropping her bag on the ground so she could gather her skirts and squeeze the water out of them. "Great. Once again, I must suffer with wet boots."

"Need I remind ye that I offered to help?"

"Nay," she snapped. "Nay ye dinnae. I remember weel enough, thank ye."

"I dinnae suppose ye packed another pair of boots in yer bag?" Rory asked, kenning full well she had not.

She rolled her eyes at him, ignoring the question. She reached down and picked up her bag, slinging it over her shoulders and gave him an exasperated look. "Weel." She sliced her hand through the air. "Shall we continue?"

Rory pressed his lips together, fighting the laugh that threatened to spill from his lips. Something he had had to do a few times since meeting Alana Duran. And not something that was in alignment with his usual countenance. Lord above she was a spitfire now, he could only imagine her ire at him if she found him laughing at her.

"Are ye for certs we are headed in the right direction?" She asked some time later.

"I will have ye ken I am kenned far and wide for my superior hiking skills," he said proudly. "Tracking skills as weel."

Again, she rolled her eyes as she clutched her hands in front of her chest in exaggeration. "Weel, then, I will keep that in mind when I am in search of a lost item."

It was his turn to roll his eyes. Damn this lass. She was irritating beyond belief. Even moreso than his sisters, all three of them, and that was saying a lot.

"Ye didnae answer my question."

He sighed in exasperation. "Aye. I ken where we are going."

They came across a large fallen tree. Rory climbed over first, and then turned and offered his hand. This time, Alana accepted it, placing her small hand in his, and he helped her over.

"How long will it take to arrive to my betrothed's lands?"

Rory shrugged. "Three days."

"Three days!" She yelled, sending the birds scampering out of the trees, taking flight for the skies. "For certs ye are taking the long route to make me suffer." Accusation laced her words.

"I am no'. I wouldnae do that. I may no' be happy aboot this task, but I will ensure to deliver ye to yer betrothed safe and sound."

"There must be a shortcut or two we can take. I cannae fathom hiking for such a long time. 'Tis unnecessary."

With his jaw clenched, he took a few calming breaths afore speaking. "That is where ye are wrong, Lady Alana. Naught good comes of a shortcut."

"I beg to differ," Alana countered. "We would arrive to our destination quicker. A win for both of us. Ye can return to yer home, and I can be left at mine without wasting time traipsing through rough landscape that is proving to be treacherous."

Rory lifted a brow. "Treacherous? To what do ye refer?"

She paused, holding out her fingers. "Let me count. One," she held out her thumb. "I fell in the burn."

"By yer own doing," he cut in.

Ignoring him, she continued, holding out her index finger. "Two, I nearly tripped o'er that fallen tree."

He barked out a laugh. He couldn't help it. "Lass, that tree was nearly as tall as ye. Ye wouldnae have tripped o'er it. Run into it? Mayhap if ye were walking with yer eyes closed," he smirked.

Crossing her arms, she glared at him. "I told ye no' to call me lass. Ye are making this journey harder than it needs to be. On purpose. I am for certs of it. What harm can come of a shortcut?"

"There is uncertainty in taking such measures to save time. Danger lurks in places off the kenned pathways. Bandits roam these parts freely. The less used a path, the more likely they are to attack there."

"Ye say ye are an expert hiker and tracker. Cannae ye track them so they dinnae attack?"

"I am no' a seer. I cannae tell the future. The best way to keep ye safe is to stay on weel-kenned roads. As I said, I will ensure yer safety. This is how I plan to do that. Sometimes a shortcut can mean death. That is no' a chance I am willing to take when I am responsible for getting ye to yer betrothed unharmed."

As dusk fell, Rory looked for a place to camp for the night. One not far off from the road, but somewhere that offered trees as a canopy in case of rain.

He paused, seeing just the spot. "We will camp here for the night," he announced. Dropping his sack onto the ground.

Alana looked around in disbelief. "Ye jest."

Shaking his head, he knelt and opened his pack. "Ye keep accusing me of jesting. If ye kenned me at all, ye would ken that I dinnae jest. 'Twill be dark soon. We cannae go on any further this night. We will sup and sleep and start again in the morn."

Standing there, Alana made no move as he set about starting a fire. He wasn't offering her comfort, but he wasn't a complete arse. He would ensure she was warm through the night, and hopefully dry out her boots, stockings, and skirts. Though her skirts appeared dry enough now, but he was for certs her stockings and boots were still wet.

With the fire built, he brought over two large stones for them to sit upon. "Sit. Ye need sustenance for tomorrow's hike." He broke the loaf of bread Tilly had packed in two and offered Alana a half. For a long moment, he didn't think she would accept, but she finally did, sitting down in a huff as she snatched the bread out of his hand.

He set a skin of ale betwixt them to share and offered her some of the dried meat Tilly had also included.

They ate in silence. Rory watched as the night grew darker, and the shadows of the flames played across Alana's face. He couldn't deny her beauty. Her future husband would have his hands full with her, but he would always have a bonny face to look upon.

After they'd finished their food, they took care of nature's call and returned to the fire. He pulled out two plaids and offered her one.

Her gaze dropped from his face to his hands and the plaid he offered and then back to him.

"Ye werenae jesting aboot sleeping on the ground?"

He held his arms out. "I wasnae. Do ye see any villages around? There are none."

"'Twill be hard and uncomfortable."

He sighed, tired of her pushback on everything they'd done today. He tossed her a plaid, not caring if she caught it or not, then unfurled his own and laid it out on the ground and settled into it.

"Ye better get used to it then." Wrapping the wool around himself, he turned on his side, facing the fire and out toward the road, ignoring Alana's huffing and puffing.

Biting back a chuckle when she finally snatched up the plaid and wrapped herself into it.

Och, a spitfire she was indeed.

❖ ━━━━━━━━━━ ❖

CHAPTER FOUR

ALANA AWAKENED WITH a jerk, groaning at the stiffness in her back, and shivered. She was freezing. Her fingers and toes were numb with cold. Slowly, she sat up, running her hands through her hair, which she had somehow managed to get pine needles and dirt mixed into it.

Lovely.

She must look a mess. Her mother would be most displeased. She could almost hear her mother's voice as she scolded her about the importance of taking care of one's appearance, especially in the presence of the opposite sex. Though she was for certs that Rory was not someone she should fash about. Once again her thoughts traveled to how her father or her husband-to-be would react when they found out how she had been mistreated by Rory Hart.

"Here." Rory offered her the skin of ale and she took a long sip. "Good morn."

"Is it?" She asked. "It doesnae feel good. As a matter of fact, it feels positively bleak." She stood and groaned as her back cracked. "I dinnae believe I have e'er slept so uncomfortably in all my life."

Rory shrugged, his eyes watching her. "We have at least one more night outside. Ye should be used to it by then."

With his boot, he stomped out the dying embers of the fire as she sat on one of the rocks and slipped on her stockings and then her boots. Thankfully, both of them had dried overnight. Hopefully, she would manage to keep herself and her clothing dry this day.

She looked up at the gray sky and frowned. The dark clouds moving lazily across the landscape didn't look promising. She feared more wet boots, stockings, and clothing were in her future.

"We should go," Rory stated impatiently as if she were delaying him.

Standing, she winced as her muscles screamed in protest. She would not let him see her discomfort. Refused to. Nay, she would carry on, maintaining her dignity and denying him the pleasure of seeing her suffer.

Holding out a piece of bread to her, she just stared at it, having the mind to refuse when her stomach betrayed her and let out a mighty growl. Snatching it out of his hand, Alana ate hurriedly as she watched Rory pick up her plaid, shake it out, and then roll it afore placing it in his pack.

Rory waited to ensure she had finished and then slipped his bag over his shoulders. She did the same, biting back the moan at the ache in her stiff shoulders. Once this journey was done, she vowed to never go on a hike again. These treks were why carriages were invented. Why horses existed.

Why she wasn't on one now still baffled her. All because Rory was put off because he'd been tasked as her escort when he had plans to hike.

He could have gone on his hike after he had delivered her to her betrothed.

Just like the day afore, Rory walked quickly, causing her to hurry her steps so she could keep up, no matter how much her body didn't want to accommodate the pace. She didn't have a choice. She truly believed if she fell behind, he would just leave her. His oath be damned.

As he slowed his steps just a wee bit, she fell in line beside him, refusing to show him any amount of weakness. She could do this. She just needed to convince her body that it was capable. The way her body kept protesting was a sign that she needed to leave the confines of her home more often and enjoy some time in the beauty of nature that surrounded her. Her home, Auchenford, wasn't set in such a beautiful backdrop as these lands offered, but it held its own beauty.

They climbed a particularly steep hill, and Alana slipped again. She was surprised when strong arms closed around her, preventing her from falling. Rory held her steady as she caught her balance, looking down at her with what looked to be genuine concern on his face. As soon as she was stable, he let go quickly, as if he'd been stung by a hundred bees.

On and on they went, the rain thankfully not arriving and saving her from another wet walk. With the ground remaining dry, she had less chance of slipping, which meant less opportunities to have to rely on Rory for help—which she refused. Nay, she would not ask for his assistance again.

Even when her feet formed blisters from the fast pace in which they walked. She remained quiet. Nary a whimper escaped her gritted teeth as she pushed forward.

They continued on with no respite, her feet painfully blistered so that she finally had to speak up. "Must we go at such a pace all day? Cannae we slow down?"

"Nay."

One word. That was all he gave her. She clenched her fists. This man was truly insufferable. Uncaring. "Ye are going too fast, and I believe ye are doing it on purpose." She finally gave in. "Are ye trying to break me?"

He paused, his back stiff and turned to her. "As ye have said more than once, my lady," he said sarcastically. "Ye are on a schedule. I am only trying to ensure ye dinnae leave yer dear betrothed waiting overlong for yer arrival." He spun and continued on.

Alana had no choice but to carry on, seething, as she glared at his back. A very broad back, she noted, but chased away the thought as soon as it entered her mind. Rory Hart was not someone she would give another thought to after this trip was said and done.

At least the clouds had finally broken up and the sun appeared, warming her skin. She took relief in that and tried to think of aught but the blisters on her feet as they continued on their journey.

She looked at the thick trees, tall and strong as they swayed in the light breeze. Listened to the birds twittering away as they passed. The squirrels chittering as they scattered, jumping from branch to branch, as she and Rory drew near. A hawk's cry in the distance. The lush green of the forest. She had to admit it was beautiful. The Highlands were like naught she had ever seen. They were so very different than where she had spent all of her life in the lowlands. The landscape there was more open with less trees. The fields were green, but there was something about being this far north that changed the colors. The green was deeper. Darker. More beautiful.

She had feared that she would miss her familial home when she had left, but the beauty of the Highlands for certs would help ease her sense of loss.

"We will stop here for a brief respite."

Alana almost cried in relief. But she didn't. To do so would show Rory how much she was struggling, and she would not allow him to see that. She wouldn't give him whatever sliver of satisfaction that he might gain from seeing her suffer. Instead, she nodded and excused herself so that she could take care of personal matters in private.

"Dinnae stray far."

She looked at him in disbelief. "Where'er would I go? I dinnae ken where we are."

His face softened, just a touch. "I only want ye to be safe is all."

"I will be certs to watch my surroundings as I relieve myself."

She rolled her eyes as she moved out of sight. Once she had, she slumped over, walking gingerly, trying to nurse her feet the best she could. She darenae remove her boots for fear that she would not be able to put them back on. She would administer to them when they stopped for the night.

How long from now would that be she couldn't ascertain. They'd been walking for quite some time today, but she was sure dusk was far from them.

Slowly, she made her way back to where Rory was leaning against a tree waiting. She straightened when she saw him, forcing herself to walk without limping.

He offered her some dried meat and ale.

This time she didn't fight him and accepted his offering.

"We have gone aboot half the distance we need today."

Half? She fought back the tears that threatened. However was she going to make it through the rest of the day?

"If ye are ready, we can push forward."

She wanted to whimper and beg for lenience but kenned it would get her nowhere. Still, she asked for a small boon to see if he would appease her. "Can we please slow our pace? Just a wee bit?"

"I am keeping the pace that will get us to yer betrothed in the allotted time. If ye cannae keep up, ye'll be left behind," he added coldly.

She sighed, closing her eyes, and tilting her head up to the sky. Why? Why did it have to be Rory Hart to escort her? Clearly, he did not want the task. And he was making her miserable on purpose. As if he was trying to prove some unkenned point. What? That she wasn't a hiker?

Aye.

He only had to ask her and she would admit to that.

For him to hold such anger against her because she delayed his planned hiking trip seemed like a dastardly thing to do. She hadn't ordered him to escort her. If aught, he should be angered with his father. He was following his orders, not hers.

Alana was beginning to think she would have been better off with the men her husband-to-be had sent to her. They hadn't taken kindly to her, that was obvious, but they hadn't made her hike.

Nay, they only abandoned ye the first chance they got.

Sighing, she ignored the stabbing pain in her feet and the blisters that were for certs growing larger with each step and hurried to catch Rory.

They moved on in silence. Alana refusing to say a word. Refusing to complain. To show weakness. She would not. But she could barely stifle her cry of relief when he finally announced they would be stopping for the night.

She did not even care that once again, they would be sleeping outside on the ground. She could only think of getting off of her feet, removing her boots and surveying the damage the days of hiking had done to them.

Just as the night afore, Rory handed her a blanket, then set about starting a fire to keep them warm for the night—and to roast the hare he'd snared.

All the while they spoke not one word to each other. Instead, they ignored each other. She found she much preferred the silence than his dismissive conversation.

Alana rolled out the plaid, laying it flat on the ground and nearly collapsed onto it. Quickly, she untied her boots, each loose of the lace took off the pressure on her feet and throbbing pain replaced the numbness she had begun to feel.

Slipping off the boots with a groan, she rolled down her stockings, the gray wool stained with blood from the blisters that had burst and the skin that had been rubbed raw.

With a wince, she dabbed at the numerous pustules covering the bottoms of her feet, the tops of her toes, and her heels with the water Rory had handed her earlier. He probably meant for her to drink it, but she couldn't right now. She needed to treat her wounds. These would take forever to heal. She for certs will be traveling with the painful abscesses for the rest of their journey.

"Here. Ye need to eat." Rory's eyes dropped to her feet and blew wide for a moment afore the uncaring mask he always wore slipped back into place.

Taking what he offered with a 'thank you', she nibbled at the meat, which he'd somehow prepared to taste quite pleasant on her tongue. Alana wasn't sure how he had managed such a feat, unless he carried a small stash of spices in his backpack. She supposed he could be. She hadn't paid any attention to what he'd brought along. She only kenned that he was much better equipped than she was.

Not for his lack of warning. He had tried. She had just refused to listen. She could acknowledge her own stubbornness.

After Alana had finished her meal, she rinsed her stockings and laid them out to dry.

Rory was propped up against a nearby tree, wrapped in his plaid as he watched the woods around them. They hadn't crossed any other travelers today, so she wasn't sure why he seemed on edge this eve.

She laid down, trying not to think about how she would manage the journey on the morrow. She kenned that she would. Failure was not an option. Showing Rory weakness was also not an option.

Reaching into her pocket, she withdrew the keepsake her mother had slipped into her hand as Alana was loaded into the carriage just afore she left Auchenford. The bauble was amber with a tiny bud of heather encompassed within. She had always admired it when it was on her mother's chest of drawers. The shorter one where she would sit in front of the looking glass whilst getting ready.

Her mother had always kept it there, in a small, round silver dish.

Now, it brought tears to her eyes. They slipped down her cheeks and wet the blanket beneath her. She missed her mother. Her father. She sniffed softly, not wanting to draw Rory's attention to her cries. She thought about her future. The reason for her arranged marriage—to provide a strong alliance for her clan. Financial safety for her family. Peace for her clan that would keep them from war. She understood the reasoning, but it didn't mean that she agreed with it.

Outwardly, aye. She would never bring shame upon her family by showing any resistance to the match. Alana would do what she had to do to keep her family safe and secure. That was the duty she had been tasked with and she would fulfill it accordingly.

But that didn't stop the tears from falling as she turned onto her side, the amber clenched in her fist.

For the briefest of moments, her eyes met Rory's. His look was softer as he assessed her, but he said naught. He only watched her, and Alana could only imagine what he was thinking.

CHAPTER FIVE

THERE WERE OFT times when Rory felt like an arse. This was one of those times. Last night, he had sat and watched Alana break down into tears.

Why?

He didn't ken. He hadn't bothered to ask. He had done naught to aid her in any way. He didn't offer comfort or speak soothing words. No solace came from him. Instead, he just sat against the tree, watching silently as she did her best to conceal her tears—until their eyes clashed. Then there was no denying the fact.

Yet still he said naught.

Even now, as he watched her quietly wrap strips of linen around her blistered feet, he said naught.

And when she winced as she slipped her boots on, her teeth gnashing at her lip to stop herself from crying out, he, once again, remained silent.

Her strength radiated from her in waves, yet he didn't acknowledge her in any way.

He was an arse of the worst variety.

Alana pushed to her feet, masking the pain she was for certs feeling and scooped up the blanket she'd slept on. Rolling it up as she walked to him with nary a limp in her step.

And he kenned she was in pain. He had no doubt. Her feet

were in an awful state.

If he were a gentleman, he would insist that they delay their journey until her feet recovered and she could continue on with no issue.

But he wasn't, so he didn't. Nay, instead, he only accepted the blanket she passed to him and turned to stuff it into his travel sack.

Once he'd snuffed out the fire with his boots, they carried forward on their journey. As much as he wanted to push through at the pace they'd done the past couple of days, he couldn't bring himself to do it. Rory found himself in awe of Alana's perseverance. Her ability to push through the pain without complaint.

Without a word actually.

She hadn't said a thing since they'd left.

Every once in a while he would steal a glance in her direction, but their eyes never met. She was always looking at something that had caught her attention—a bird, a tree. Hell, a bug. Aught but him.

And through it all, he could see the tense of her jaw, and kenned she was clenching her teeth as she kept moving.

"I need refreshment," he announced, and Alana paused. He didn't. Not really. But guilt—an emotion he didn't feel very often—had slowly been building, and he felt that he should give her a respite, even if only for a brief moment. "Ale?" He asked, handing her the skin he'd pulled from his side.

She paused so long that he expected her to refuse his offering, but she finally nodded and reached for the drink, taking a long pull. Good. Mayhap the ale would lessen the bite of pain she was enduring.

"Thank ye. Ye didnae have to stop on my account. I am perfectly fine to move on without delay." Her voice was clipped as she spoke. "I ken ye are anxious to arrive to our destination and divest yerself of my presence."

Rory frowned, biting the inside of his cheek. 'Twas true that he wanted this journey to be done with as quickly as possible, but when she had confronted him with the words that were whirling in his mind, guilt once again flowed over him. He realized that he hadn't denied her statement. "Now that we are in the thick of the forest, I find myself no' as anxious as afore." He gave her a sincere smile, something he didn't give freely or often. "Nature has a way of healing my anger."

She harrumphed but said naught.

"Do ye want more?" He pointed to the skin she was still holding.

Her eyes dropped to her hands as she lifted the ale. It was as if she had forgotten that she still held it and shook her head. She held out her hand so he could take the skin back and secure it to his side.

"If yer thirst needs quenching at any time whilst we travel, ye only need let me ken and we will stop."

Alana didn't answer, only looked off through the trees.

He sighed and held his hand out in front of him, signaling the direction they needed to continue in.

"Is that water I hear? Crashing aboot it sounds like." Alana asked.

"Aye. 'Tis falls that are no' too far from here."

"Falls?" She questioned.

"Aye. The Falls of Fae arenae far from here. The water passing over them is strong which is why ye can hear it at this distance. Would ye like to see them?" The question left his lips afore he could stop them. He wanted to kick himself. Whilst he had resigned himself to the fact that they were taking longer to arrive at the MacDonell clan than he had anticipated, veering off path to visit the falls was more time wasted than he wanted.

"What a unique name."

"They are legendary. The fae have spent centuries watching o'er the falls. 'Tis said at cert times of the year one can get close enough to the fae here that ye can see them."

"Have ye e'er seen them?"

He shook his head and chuckled. "I havenae. Though I have

been here oft enough. I guess I dinnae have the right qualities they seek."

Her forehead crinkled in confusion. "They seek something?"

"Mostly, they want to be left alone. They seek the peace and quiet of the land. But they enjoy offerings. Flowers, stones, baubles. They take them back to their palace to decorate its walls."

Alana's breath hitched. "Have ye seen their castle?"

"Nay. I have no' been blessed enough to be granted that luxury."

"Then how do ye ken it truly exists?"

He hadn't realized the fae would have enraptured Alana so. Did they not have fae in the lowlands? He had never thought about it, but it seemed they would be in all locations. Whilst the highlands offered much protection, it surely could not be the only place they were found.

"I have heard the tales. They are passed on from generation to generation."

She cocked her head to the side as she studied him, her lips pressed together. "I think I would like to see," she said finally after a long silence.

"We are a little higher than the mid-way point of the falls. The true magic is seen from the top. This way."

He led them through the thick trees, slowly climbing higher and higher. He didn't have his climbing gear, and even if he had, Alana was ill-equipped to partake in such a feat, especially with the wounds on her feet, so he slowly circled them up and around, taking them even longer.

"Almost there," Rory announced as they emerged from the trees. The sounds of rushing water filled the air around them. "We just need to make our way over this ledge and then ye will see the most breathtaking sight ye have e'er laid yer eyes upon," he promised.

Her gaze went to the high ledge and he could see the uncertainty in her eyes. "Dinnae fash. I will help ye climb it."

She gave a subtle shake of her head.

"I have climbed it many a time. 'Tis no' as difficult as it appears. I'll show ye." He clasped her hand and pulled her forward, ignoring the heat that emanated up his wrist and arm from their entwined fingers. "Look," he pointed to the ledge. "There are notches in the rock that make it easy to climb. Ye are only a few steps away from the top."

"There must be another way to get to the top," she stated, and Rory shook his head.

"Nay, this is the only way." He shifted so he could look her in the eyes. "I promise ye I willnae let any harm come to ye. All will be well, I assure ye" He caressed her hand with the pad of his thumb.

He didn't understand why he cared so much whether or not she made the climb. But he found himself holding his breath as he waited for her answer.

The corners of his mouth lifted when she finally nodded.

"Put yer foot here." He pointed to the first notch. "Wait. That willnae work." He rubbed his chin as he thought for a moment. What was the best approach to get them up there together? He could have her rest his feet on his and he could make the steps, but once they reached near the top, he wouldn't be able to assist her getting over the lip. He would have to go first and guide her through.

"The best way to get ye up there, is if I climb up first. Then ye follow my instructions on where to put yer feet. Once ye are close enough to the top, I can lift ye the rest of the way."

She eyed him cautiously, her teeth worrying her bottom lip, afore looking around at their surroundings. "How do I ken ye willnae abandon me here?"

"Hey." He tipped her chin up with his finger so their eyes could meet. "Whye'er would I bring ye all this way only to leave ye alone?"

Alana shrugged. "Ye wouldnae be the first to do so."

The words she spoke hurt, hitting him right in the heart. She had been put through a trial this past sennight. And all for duty to her family. Rory admired her dedication, but he was sad to see the toll it was taking on the lass.

Her eyes shined with unshed tears. She was scared. Frightened to be left alone. He may be an arse, but he would never do such a thing.

"Look at me. Am I happy to make this journey? As I have said, nay. I have no qualms admitting to that. But I have a duty. An honor to escort ye safely to yer destination. I fulfill my duties—always. And that doesnae include leaving ye to fend for yerself alone in the woods."

Alana's shoulders sagged in relief.

"Now, let us climb this ledge afore we anger the fae and they appear and create havoc."

Her eyes widened. "Is that what they do?"

He chuckled. "I have ne'er been given the chance to find out. I have only heard the stories. But let us no' test that theory." He bent so their gazes were at the same level. "Agreed?"

She nodded.

"Right. Watch where I step into the notches. Ye will need to do the same for the first few. After that, I can pull ye up the rest of the way."

Her teeth pulled at her lip, but she nodded.

He made quick work of the climb, speaking the whole time. Letting Alana ken exactly what he was doing and why. Once he was atop, he laid on his stomach and hung his hands down. "Hold on to the bumps in the rock, then put yer right foot in the lowest notch. Yer left foot in the next one." He paused, waiting. Watching.

Alana was pure concentration, her tongue tucked into the corner of her mouth. An action that was affecting Rory's body in the most unsuspecting way that he was taken off guard. And his mind. Visions of the two of them climbing and hiking through the Highlands flooded his mind. Distracting him. So much so, that when Alana had done as she was told, she had to ask him what to do next. His body and his mind had betrayed him. Why? Why here? Why *her*? It wasn't something he could dwell on now.

"Move yer hands up and grasp the next bumps. Dinnae look down," he added quickly as he noticed what she was going to do. He was unsure if heights made her stomach turn, but he didn't want to find out in the middle of her climbing a ledge because he wouldn't be able to stop her from falling. "Keep yer eyes focused on the ledge or me. That's it. Ye can drag yer foot up and yer boot will find the next notch. Good. Now do the same with yer left foot."

She was gritting her teeth and he kenned it was from the pain of the blisters on her feet. Even though she had wrapped them this morn, the wrapping would only protect the wounds from further irritation, but did naught for the pain.

"Only one more sequence of steps and then ye will be close enough for me to pull ye up the rest of the way."

Alana nodded and repeated the steps she had done moments afore. Once she finished he reached out to her. "Give me yer hand."

Alana's gaze clashed with his. Fierceness blazed in the depths of her hazel eyes. Brilliant pools that held flecks of amber and threatened to suck him in. To trap him in their whirlpool and drag him under. Rory took a deep breath to clear his mind.

Her hand reached out to his, her fingertips grazing his, before she cried out and grasped the bump in the rock. "I cannae reach. Ye are too far."

Moving further over the ledge, he urged her to try again. "Listen to me?" He said gently, locking his eyes with hers.

She nodded.

"Take my hand." He gestured it toward her, fingers splayed, palm out.

Biting her lip, she swung her hand up, and this time Rory closed his hand over hers with a smile. "Now yer other one." She did as she was told and he pulled her up. The lass was light as a feather and the task was easy enough.

Once he had her over his shoulder, she scrambled over him and onto the flat surface of the ledge, breathing heavily. They stood at the same time, and she lost her footing. Her eyes wide as she began to fall backward, clutching at his arm, panic clear on her face.

He moved quickly, grasping her shoulders, and pulling her in toward him.

She didn't scream and once again, he found himself in awe of her strength.

Steadying her, he noted her shaking hands, but also the way she held her chin high as if saying that she meant to do that. That she was only testing him.

She was so convincing, that he almost believed it.

Now that she wasn't in any danger of falling over the ledge, she walked to the other side where the Falls of Fae burst forth from an opening in the mountain. Its water gushing out and spilling over and down the long path of the mountain side to finally pool in the crystal blue waters below.

Her breath caught at the sight and he kenned she found it just as beautiful as he did. It was in the way she took the scene in front of her in. Her eyes studying the opening where the water came through, then lowering, falling, falling, falling until they looked at the water below.

She noticed him staring and quickly masked her true feelings.

He didn't say aught. He understood. He was the master of masking his feelings. How coincidental it was that she did the same.

"Have ye e'er swam below?"

"Nay," He shook his head.

"Why no'? It looks beautiful."

"Aye, 'tis." He shrugged his shoulders and pulled on the back of his neck. "I dinnae ken. I didnae want to upset the fae."

Her eyes wandered over the landscape, and she nodded. "It does feel bewitching here. As if an unseen pull is tugging at me."

He nodded. He kenned the feeling. "I feel it, too. 'Tis the

same e'ery time I am here."

"And ye've ne'er seen them?"

He shook his head. "Nay, no' once."

They lingered there for some time afore making their way back down the ledge. That took more urging to get Alana to agree to come down than it did to get her to climb up.

She breathed a sigh of relief once she was on solid ground again. "Thank ye for showing me that. I ken it was a waste of time for ye, but I appreciate the gesture."

Her words affected him more than they should. So much so, that he only nodded and led her in the direction they needed to go. He didn't want to admit that he enjoyed the delay. Enjoyed seeing her reaction to the world of beauty that he saw in his beloved Highlands.

The trek to the Falls had set them further behind schedule and they had to stop and spend another night under the stars. As they shared a meal, Rory found himself studying Alana. She was a strong woman. He could see that in the way she held her head high, her chin notched up just a wee bit, showing that she wasn't only strong, but possessed a stubborn streak as well.

Something they had in common for certs.

"What of yer betrothed? Did he truly only send two guards to escort ye to his home?" The words were out of his mouth afore he could stop them. He noted the way her eyes darkened at the mention of the man that would be her husband. Rory couldn't imagine only sending two guards for such an important task. What was MacDonell thinking? Did the man not care for his wife-to-be?

Rory could only conclude that he did not. Otherwise, he would have taken more care. Anger bubbled in his chest. Did the dolt not recognize the danger or did he truly not care?

"Originally, he sent two. When my father insisted I be pro-tected by more men than that on the journey our trip was delayed for some days whilst more guards were sent. My father offered our men, but they were refused." She shrugged. "Once we were past Auchenford's gates and out of sight, the men scattered, leaving me with the two that were sent to begin with." With a sigh, she picked up the skin of ale and took a long pull, her eyes staring out into the darkness of the trees surrounding them.

He wondered what she was thinking. "I mean nay disrespect, but I must say the man is a fool."

Her gaze swung to his and she worried her bottom lip with her teeth as her eyes roamed over his face.

"Thank ye." The words slipped past her lips so quietly he almost didn't hear them. And from her reaction to saying them, she seemed surprised herself.

Later that night, he caught himself staring at her as shadows from the firelight danced across her features. The flames making her dark hair shimmer in the night.

His thoughts wandered to a place that they shouldn't and he tore his gaze away, focusing on the night sky and the stars twinkling above them. He had no right thinking such thoughts.

Alana Duran was just a job. A mission Rory had been tasked with. That was all. Naught more.

It was something he would need to remind himself often if he wanted to complete this task unattached with his heart intact.

CHAPTER SIX

Rory had sat awake for a long time after Alana had laid down and curled into her plaid. She hadn't been able to sleep and she couldn't understand why. It had been a trying day. She'd walked for what seemed like miles. Climbed that ledge—she wouldn't even think about how terrified she was—or how she felt when Rory's strong hands wrapped around her arms to steady her.

Nay, she would not give that a second thought.

She could not. She had no right even allowing such things to enter her mind. Not when she was promised to another.

Listening to Rory's soft snores as he slept just feet from her on the other side of the fire had a strange pang pulling at her gut. She took comfort that through his rough and hard exterior he seemed to truly care for her safety.

More than once she'd caught him watching her. Normally, that would instill fear or uneasiness in her. She didn't like the attention of men—her father excluded, of course. But when Rory Hart stared at her, it ignited a heat deep within her belly.

Even now as she watched him, she wanted to reach over and sweep the curl of hair that had fallen onto his forehead, covering his eye. She wanted to run her finger along the deep scar on his left cheek. The shadows from the fire made it appear even deeper, adding to her intrigue. She wondered what happened to cause such a wound. Its edges were slightly roughened, not a complete straight scar, but close. It could have been done by a blade or something else equally as sharp. The possibilities were endless. She had seen her brothers injure themselves enough to ken that the cause could be aught.

The annoyance she had felt when they'd first been thrust together on this journey had been slowly dissipating. It began to be replaced. By what? She dared not voice the words. Naught good could come of it.

She was betrothed to another. Someone she had never met. Still, she tried to form an image of him in her mind. To conjure his face. But each time she did, it was always Rory looking back at her.

⇥⟫⟩✕⟨⟪⇤

THE NEXT MORN after they'd cleaned their camp and broke their fast on dried fruit and the last of their bread, Rory offered his hand and helped Alana to her feet. Her still pained feet, but the pain was less this morn. It helped that the day afore, they moved at a much slower pace, and she had kept her feet dry. The swelling had gone down this morn and it was much easier to get her boots on. Even so, she had still wrapped her feet. She was for certs doing so the morn afore had played a large part in how her feet were feeling today.

"What shall I carry?" She asked, her voice sounding overly jovial even to her own ears.

Rory lifted a brow as he pondered her question and she believed she saw his lips tick up a wee bit at the corners of his mouth.

"I can be of assistance, ye ken. I am stronger than I look. I am no' a weakling if that is what ye are thinking."

He raised his hands in defense. "'Tis no' what I was thinking at all. I ken ye are strong," he admitted, and she couldn't ignore the way his confession made her stomach tumble. He lifted his shoulders in a shrug. "If ye would like to help, ye can carry this."

Unhooking the roll of blankets from his pack, he fastened them to hers and helped her slip the pack on her shoulders.

"Too heavy?" He asked.

She rolled her eyes. "These weigh naught."

"But they are bulky. If they are too much, I will take them back." His brows furrowed.

Did he really think she was so incompetent? The thought irritated her. She gave him a quick shake of her head and waited for him to load up the rest of their items.

Then she assessed his reaction. He hadn't acted as if he believed she couldn't carry them. Nay, instead, he seemed affronted in some way. As if she had insulted him. Alana rolled her eyes again, a gesture she found herself doing quite often in Rory's presence, as she walked beside him, realizing that she had taken away his chivalry. He wanted to carry everything. Having her do so was taking away his manhood, or whatever it was that was going on inside his head.

She dipped her head to hide her smile.

Rory Hart, deep down inside, was a chivalrous man. She wanted to giggle.

Giggle!

She couldn't remember the last time she had done so.

They walked on, side by side, quietly, as a strange peace settled betwixt them.

A contentment that she hadn't felt in a long time consumed her.

They approached a fast-moving burn and Rory suggested they stop for a respite. Him doing so was so different from the man she had first begun this journey with. That man hadn't wanted to stop for aught. He just wanted to push through everything. But not this one.

This one was caring. Concerned.

And she wasn't sure what to do with that realization.

As Rory bent over the burn, splashing the cool water over his face, she noticed a hare hop from the screen of the bushes.

She couldn't call out to Rory for fear of frightening the animal away. His bow was close.

And if there was aught that Alana could do, it was shoot an arrow with exact precision, a skill she had kept to herself. Keeping her body still, and her eyes on the hare, she moved her hand slowly until her fingers closed around the bow, bringing it to her, then did the same as she plucked an arrow from the quiver.

The hare came further forth from the bushes cautiously, pausing every couple of seconds to assess its surroundings.

Moving quietly, she notched the arrow and closing her left eye, she focused her right eye on the target. Inhaling, she let the arrow loose, watching it connect with deadly precision.

Behind her Rory gasped in surprise.

"Impressive shot. Where did ye learn to shoot an arrow like that?"

Was that pride she heard in his voice?

She shrugged. "My brothers. They thought it could be a helpful skill to have if I ever found myself lost in the forest. Dinnae tell my mother or father. They would be mortified to learn of me doing such an unladylike thing."

"Weel, my lips are sealed, and yer brothers were right. With aim like that, ye will for certs no' go hungry." He smiled at her. A genuine smile that crinkled the corners of his eyes and made the green sparkle like emeralds.

She froze, caught off-guard by his compliment, unsure of what to say. It wasn't aught that she expected to hear from him, and she didn't want to admit how much it affected her.

Later, as they prepared the hare together for their meal, side by side, they were so close she could feel the heat emanating off his body.

A brush of his fingers against her skin, lingering a smidge too long to be considered decent. His lip caught betwixt his teeth as their eyes met.

Alana pulled away quickly, breaking the connection and Rory took a step back, shaking his head, as if awakening himself from a stupor.

What were they doing? If someone happened upon them, they would for certs think they were more than a woman and her guard.

Her skin still tingled where his fingers had touched her. She fought the urge to rub the spot, not wanting to draw attention to how much it affected her.

She had to remind herself that it was naught. That it couldn't ever be aught. She was betrothed to another man. She had a duty to her family. She couldn't forget that.

She needed to repeat it over and over.

Rory was not her future.

He couldn't be.

Ever.

But when he gave her a bright smile. A smile that held promises she kenned that he had no right making, her heart stumbled.

They supped in silence, away from each other on opposites side of the fire they'd roasted the prepared hare over. Alana sat cross-legged on her blanket, pulling the tender meat from the bone with her fingers. They stole glances the whole time and averted their eyes as soon as they made contact.

She felt silly. It was like she was playing the childhood games that she'd played as a young girl. But she wasn't a young girl any longer and Rory was definitely not a young boy.

And the game they were playing was most definitely not child's play.

Nay. He was all man. Big and tall. Dark and brooding. Protective and sincere. True to his word.

She had witnessed that firsthand. Rory and no qualms telling her how much he despised having to put his plans on hold to escort her to her betrothed. He had reminded her oft enough. Yet, he also took pride in himself and the way he treated her. He got angry on her behalf at learning the details of her circumstances.

Aye, there were times when he was short and dare she say, rude. He had threatened to leave her behind, but even when she hadn't kenned him well, she kenned he would do no such thing.

Alana sighed over a nibble of roasted meat.

Rory raised a brow in question but didn't say a word.

But when they settled in for the night, still on either side of the fire, and his deep voice wished her a good sleep, his warm tone like a soft blanket, Alana's heart skipped a beat and she couldn't hide the smile that lifted her lips.

CHAPTER SEVEN

Rory and Alana had been walking for a few hours already. They had left just after daybreak since they'd both awakened early. The air was heavy and he kept an eye on the sky above as the fat clouds, thick with rain, moved over them, threatening them with a good drenching.

A right *dreich* day it was. He quickened their pace, hoping to beat the rain and seek shelter inside an abandoned croft that he kenned wasn't too far from here.

But his efforts were all for naught. Within minutes, the rain was coming down hard and fast, soaking them to the bone.

Rory scanned the trees. The croft was close. He could just see the outline of the thatch roof through the fat drops falling from the sky, landing in heavy plops on his head.

"This way." He grabbed Alana's arm and pulled her forward.

"Where are we going?"

"Someplace dry," he roared over the loud rain.

With hurried steps they approached the croft, but as it came into view, Alana pulled on him to slow down.

"What is amiss?"

She pointed to the abandoned building and shook her head. "I am no' going in there."

He clenched his jaw. "'Twill keep us protected from the storm. We'll stay dry and be warm. I can start a fire." He opened his arms. "We can dry our clothes."

Her eyes darted to the croft and back to his, her teeth chattering as she began to shiver.

"Ye're freezing, lass. Ye need shelter."

"Nay, I refuse to—"

Lightning flashed overhead and within seconds thunder boomed. Alana shrieked and grasped at his arm. He pushed her inside and she let him, but quickly turned to him, her nose wrinkled up in disgust.

He ignored how cute she looked with her face scrunched up and her wet hair hanging in strands framing her bonny face.

"'Tis freezing in here," she declared, rubbing her hands up and down her arms to warm herself up.

Barring the door, he dropped his pack by the entry and moved to the hearth so he could build a fire. Luckily, the last person that had occupied the croft had left wood and kindling in the wire basket beside the hearth. Also, a bucket of pine needles and a hardened mound of sap. With all of those, he'd be able to build a hearty fire in no time and since the space wasn't overly large, it should warm up quickly.

"Take yer pack off and get out of those wet clothes afore ye catch yer death. I willnae have ye die on my watch."

"No' only is it cold in here, it smells of must and stagnation."

"As abandoned crofts do."

"I cannae stay here." Disgust dripped from her words.

Lightning crackled across the sky, lighting the space up for a brief moment and Alana jumped.

"We havenae any other choice unless ye want to be out there with the storm."

She harrumphed but began to pull items out of her pack. Trying dry herself off with the few items that hadn't soaked through, she continued to complain.

Frustrated, he turned his attention back to starting the fire, mumbling to himself about how ungrateful she was being. "Mayhap yer betrothed should just come and fetch ye himself."

"Pardon?" Alana snapped.

Rory finished blowing on the small flame. "I believe ye heard me just fine."

"Weel, we wouldnae be in this situation if ye hadnae dragged me into this disgusting place."

He stood quickly and stalked to where she stood with her hands on her hips, and towered over her. His stance forced her to crane her neck so she could look him in the eye.

"Ye are welcome to go back outside. I willnae stop ye." He jabbed his finger toward the door.

She crossed her arms defiantly. "Ye have a duty to protect me."

He wet his lips, nodding. "Aye, I do. But if ye are going to be stubborn and ungrateful and insist ye will be better off someplace other than in a dry shelter in the middle of a raging storm, then dinnae let me hold ye back."

He spun and returned to the fire, poking at the wee flames that began to sputter. Blowing on them, he added kindling and broke off a piece of sap, throwing it onto the pile with a sizzle.

Refusing to look back at her, he kenned she wouldn't leave. But when he heard her sniffle, guilt consumed him. He should apologize. He hadn't meant to be so harsh with her, but she was frustrating. Infuriating really. Stubborn and pig-headed in her ways.

"Ye ken I am only doing my duty to my family. I dinnae ken how many times I have to apologize for taking ye away from yer planned hike. That instead of having the freedom to spend yer days as ye wish, ye are stuck here with me. But 'twasnae my suggestion."

He laughed bitterly. "Nay, ye only insisted that someone appear and escort ye to yer betrothed."

Looking back, Rory saw Alana snap her mouth shut.

Aye, she couldn't deny that fact. He'd heard from the villagers. And his da as well. Alana was quite demanding when her carriage had crashed.

"Ye have nay right to sit there and judge me. Ye arenae in my boots. Ye ken naught of what demands have been placed upon my shoulders." Her narrowed eyes bore into him.

Rory scoffed. "Ye ken naught of hardship. All that ye have has been given to ye. Showered upon ye."

Alana laughed in disbelief. "Ye dinnae ken me at all. If ye did, ye would ken that was no' true. Ye speak of duty. Of honor. Yet ye arenae acting verra honorable in this moment, Rory Hart," she spat.

Her use of his full name took him aback. This argument was serving no benefit to either of them. But her passionate fight was stirring up something within him that he didn't want to acknowledge.

Tension hung thick in the air as they stared at each other.

He pushed from the floor and stalked toward her. Planting her feet, she crossed her arms and watched his every step, her mouth set into a firm line, her head cocked to the side.

They were so close. Rory only need to straighten his fingers and he would be curling a tendril of her rain-soaked hair around his hand. Her chest heaved with heavy breaths as anger seeped from every pore in her body. Her cheeks tinged pink.

He wondered what it would be like to pull her close to him. To feel her body mold against his. He kenned it would fit perfectly.

Neither of them moved. They stood in front of each other in a silent stand-off. A duel of emotions being fought betwixt them.

Lightning flashed, and Alana jumped. In the brief illumination, Rory saw another emotion on her face. Not anger. But fiery passion of a different sort.

It mirrored his own look, he was for certs.

One step.

That's all it would take.

One step and he could wrap her in his arms.

He took a step, but it wasn't forward, it was backward. And with that step, he crossed his arms as his gaze clashed with hers.

He clenched his jaw, irritation flowing through him at the onslaught of conflicting feelings running through his veins and preventing him from thinking rationally.

Dropping into the chair, he broke their eye contact and turned his attention to the fire, which was now burning brightly, heating up the small space.

She settled on the bed, shoulders straight, her eyes also focused on the flames licking up the sides of the hearth.

He didn't ken how long they stayed that way. Listening to the rage of the storm as it beat against the roof and battered against the walls. A constant rhythm that eventually lulled him into contentment, along with the sounds of the crackling fire.

Whether it did the same to Alana, he couldn't be sure. He did notice that her breathing had calmed, and she had relaxed her shoulders so she wasn't sitting as stiffly as afore.

He would take that as a good omen. Even if his own mind was conflicted with what was actually happening betwixt them. Of how she could make him so fiercely angry and so desperately long for her touch at the same time. If he were home at Hartsmoor, it would be a conversation he would have with his older brother, Alpin. The man was currently engaged to be married. He would for certs have some advice for Rory on how to handle this situation.

But since Rory was alone, he would have to navigate whatever was going on betwixt them on his own. One thing he could honestly say with no regret—if Alana was his betrothed, not only would he not send a measly two guards to escort her to her new home, he would lead the charge himself—with a whole team of men.

CHAPTER EIGHT

Aʟᴀɴᴀ sᴛᴀʀᴇᴅ ɪɴᴛᴏ the flickering firelight, her blanket pulled tightly up to her chin. She had moved to the chair Rory had found hidden in the corner and moved closer to the fire so she could sit and warm her cold toes. Around the croft, Rory worked furiously reinforcing the walls and windows to ensure the rain and wind couldn't sweep through the cracks and negate the warmth the hearth was providing.

She watched him silently, tracking his movements and trying to understand the complex man he was proving to be. For every positive trait she could identify within him, she could pair it with a negative. Her mother had always told her that men were simple creatures. As long as they had good food and a good lass warming their bed, they were happy.

Alana had hardly believed her mother when she'd told her such things afore. Her own father never really seemed happy—and Lord kenned that he always had a warm bed, and oft times it wasn't her mother joining him there.

Personally, Alana found it disrespectful, but her mother always said it was the way of things. It made him happy and that was all that mattered. But what of her mother's happiness? Did that not matter?

Even then, Alana kenned that was not the type of marriage she wanted. If she were to be wed, she wanted it to be to a loyal husband. One that only saw her. One that loved her for who she was. One that would accept her faults. She kenned she was asking for a lot. That her father was acting normally for men of certain standing. But Alana didn't agree with his actions.

Was it too much to ask to be loved? To be cherished in a way that no other would be when her husband laid eyes upon her.

She let out an audible sigh.

"'Twould seem ye are thinking hard o'er there," Rory quipped as he packed bark into a crack in the wall near the door. "Do ye want to speak of it?"

She studied him. The anomaly that was Rory Hart. He was quite insightful for someone that seemed to be so nonchalant and aloof as he moved about the croft.

He saw everything.

"Nay. No' really," she answered quietly, gently rocking to and fro, a wee squeak sounding from the old chair with every forward motion. The noise breaking up the constant howl of the wind and pounding rain.

Once again, she puzzled over Rory as she watched him move about. Despite his gruffness, the things he had done for her showed a different side of him. A caring side that he guarded ferociously. He'd taken her cloak and set it to hang on the iron hooks by the hearth so it would dry. He'd turned his back so she could strip out of her wet clothes and slip into the few dry items she had. Then he'd hung the wet items to dry as well.

He had fetched her blanket and handed it to her, urging her toward the rocking chair. He rummaged through the small cupboard in the corner and came away with tea leaves that he steeped in water that he had boiled on the hearth in a small pot he'd also located.

He handed her the tea when it was ready and then set back to work.

His kindness and caring shining through like a beacon in the darkest of nights.

The way he'd shielded her when they were outside. Even as

she refused to enter the croft. Even as she complained about the state of the croft. The musty smell. The patience he'd shown her would have never been granted in her own home.

She shook her head, a scoff falling from her lips.

He must think she was spoiled.

She kenned he did. Their heated words earlier had stung. They still did.

While her father was not the most attentive father to her, Alana had never wanted for aught. If he didn't provide what she asked, her brothers tripped over themselves to fulfill her wish. So, she supposed in that sense, she was spoiled.

Even so, she thought she had handled her current predicament well. All the hiking. The walking. The climbing. Sleeping outside on the bare ground.

None of that was aught that she was accustomed to.

But Rory? He loved all of those things. He lived for them. Breathed for them. It was as if the Highlands coursed through his blood.

"Why do ye like the Highlands so much?" She asked. Suddenly, the urge to ken and understand him better hit her strong. She wanted to ken his likes and dislikes. His dreams and desires.

Rory paused, his hand pushing against another crack he had just filled. He turned and leaned against the wall, studying her. His green eyes dark in the firelight. After a long hesitation he said, "'Tis their beauty. I set my eyes upon the land around me and 'tis the most beautiful thing I have e'er seen. As a lad, I was always outdoors. With four siblings, the castle could get loud, especially with e'erything else happening within. If I was outside, I didn't have to hear any of that. I could take my leave and venture into the forest. Climb the trees. Swim in the loch. Climb the mountains." He smiled wistfully, his eyes distant, staring off out the window.

"No one expected aught from me." He shrugged. "I'm the second brother. All the responsibility fell upon my older brother, Alpin's, shoulders. Outside, surrounded by nature, listening to the tweets of the birds, the hoots of the howls, the cries of the hawks, I felt blissfully alone. The splash of fish in the loch when I swam was a welcome sight. The scents of pine and heather blanketed me in a warm hug." He huffed out a laugh. "It probably sounds silly to ye."

"It doesnae," she said hurriedly, straightening in the chair. "Yer descriptions sound lovely, actually. Where I am from, the trees are fewer, the land more barren. And I am usually tucked safely inside of my home."

"I am for certs there is beauty to be found there as weel. Though 'tis no' as green and lush as the Highlands," he smiled teasingly, and Alana's heart ticked a wee bit faster at his look.

"Ye are right. I have to admit, the landscape here is," she paused, searching for the right word. One that would encapsulate the full description of what she was thinking. "'Tis breathtaking," she said finally.

A huge smile broke out on his face, making his eyes twinkle in the firelight. He acted as if she had just given him the greatest of compliments. "Now ye are understanding. Breathtaking is the perfect word for these lands and why I love them so. What do ye miss aboot yer home?"

The question caught her off guard. It was unexpected and she didn't think he was interested in her and the things she liked.

"The openness of the land. The sky that goes on and on with no end in sight. 'Tis calm, predictable. Which my life was until no' that long ago. My betrothal? That was aught but predictable."

He pushed off the wall and approached her. Reaching out a hand, he tenderly tucked a loose tendril of hair behind her ear, letting his fingers linger on her jawline, causing her to shiver. "That must have come as a shock for ye."

Worrying her lip betwixt her teeth, she broke their gaze and nodded. "'Twasnae aught that I could have predicted. I had ne'er thought my father would do such a thing. Or that my mother would agree to such a union. The day I found out, it stung as if I had been slapped."

Rory frowned, his eyes darkening. "I dinnae think that parents should use their children as bargaining tools."

Alana chewed the inside of her cheek afore answering. "Daughters are good for naught more than that."

His eyes snapped to hers. "Dinnae say such things. Ye are worthy of much more than that."

She shook her head. "To my family and my clan, I am no'," she said sadly. She didn't make the admission to garner his sympathy. She was only stating that she understood her position.

Taking her hands in his, he pulled her up to standing. The blanket slipped down as she stood, but Rory being the perfect gentleman didn't let his eyes roam below her face. She was fully clothed, and all her most private parts were covered, but the smock she wore was thin and she was for certs that he would be able to see the outline of her body through the material.

"I would ne'er want my daughter to have such an outlook on life. She will ken her worth and 'twillnae be how I can use her as a bargaining chip."

His words meant so much to her in that moment. Tears threatened. Without thinking, she wrapped her arms around his waist in a hug. For the briefest passage of time, Rory stiffened against her, but then relaxed and surrounded her with his warmth as he returned her embrace, resting his chin on her head. His huge arms engulfed her. In that moment she felt treasured. Protected. Safe.

They stood that way for a long time. Not moving. Just enjoying the moment of the strength of each other's arms.

Later, as they settled into the one bed the croft offered, they laid closer than ever, but didn't touch. Not yet.

What was she thinking?

Not yet.

Not ever.

She and Rory could never be together. Whilst she may not ken all that being laird entailed, and the decisions that, as laird, her father needed to make. However, she was for certs that defying this order would not only condemn her clan to poverty and leave them unprotected from attack, but it would also bring harm to the Hart clan. Or worse yet, war. She would not be the cause of any such ramifications.

As Alana drifted off to sleep feeling safe, warm, and content, she kenned that the feelings she was beginning to harbor for Rory would not be easy to forget.

And she didn't ken how she was going to survive when he left her on the doorstep of her betrothed and walked out of her life forever.

CHAPTER NINE

RORY WOKE AT dawn the next morn. Opening his eyes, he watched Alana as she slept. She was facing him, long eyelashes sweeping her cheeks, her full lips slightly apart, her chestnut hair splayed across the pillow. An unfamiliar pang hit him. One that made him want to wake up to this same scene every morn.

"Shite," he mumbled under his breath.

He had no right longing for such things. But his heart wouldn't listen. Instead it kept conjuring more images for him to see. Scenarios for him to wish for.

If their circumstances had been different, Rory could see a future with Alana. If they had met at a Highland gathering or *ceilidh,* mayhap they would find themselves in a very different situation. He could see himself drawn to her from across the room. He could imagine the pull of her making his feet move to approach her and ask her to join him in a dance. He had never been much of a dancer, but for Alana he would make an exception. That alone told him he was letting himself be drawn in by her far deeper than he should.

Never afore had he had dreams of settling down with a woman. *Dancing* with a woman. He wished he could seek guidance from Alpin. His brother would tell him whether he was daft to even consider such things or if he was scared of the commitment.

The thought had entered his mind. Not that he jumped from bed to bed. He did not. He preferred his days spent in solace. Was he scared of sharing his peace?

He took a deep breath and scrubbed his hands roughly over his face—to wake him up and to clear his mind from the errant thoughts that would serve him no purpose.

Mayhap Alana had bewitched him. It was the only explanation he could find plausible.

"Good morn," Alana mumbled shyly, her lids still heavy with sleep, her voice low.

"Good morn," Rory answered in a clipped voice. "I gather ye slept weel?"

"Aye." Her arms popped out from under the blanket and she stretched, her fingers brushing against his chest.

He stiffened, and Alana didn't seem to notice what she'd done as she withdrew her hand. He was thankful he had worn a tunic to bed. Though the thought to go to sleep bare-chested never crossed his mind. To do so would have been disrespectful, and he would do no such thing.

Her eyes went to the window and she cocked her head.

"The rain has stopped?" She asked.

"Aye," he answered as he swung his legs off the bed and pushed himself up to stand, stretching his back as he did so. "We should ready ourselves and continue on our way."

Thirty minutes later, their sacks were packed, and they exited the croft. Outside the ground was littered with leaves, pine needles, and branches that had fallen from the force of the rain and wind from the night afore.

"E'erything is amiss. The storm must have raged on e'en harder than I thought," Alana said, adding, "I am glad ye found us shelter, Rory." She placed a hand on his arm, and he straightened stiffly. "I ken I was acting most difficult when we had first arrived, but I realize that ye were doing so for our safety. Ye are a kind man."

Rory scoffed, but nodded, trying not to show how much her

touch affected him. He cleared his throat and straightened his shoulders. Whatever feelings he had thought he started to feel this morn and his reaction to Alana's recent statement irritated him. What the hell was he doing?

Alana was promised to another. He was her escort.

Her escort to her betrothed no less.

He needed to clear his head and get his mind straight. Doing so meant that he could not give allowance to the thoughts he had pondered this morn. Nay, he had no right conjuring up those images in his mind from earlier. Clenching his jaw, he vowed to keep Alana at arm's length. To not let her in. He would not. He could not.

The ground below their feet was saturated and made squishy sounds as they walked away from the croft. "The path will be slick and slippery. Dangerous e'en. We will need to take care to ensure ye dinnae fall and hurt yerself," Rory warned.

A gust of wind swirled around them, and Alana brushed her hair out of her face and nodded.

Cautiously, they ventured on, leaving the croft far behind. They approached a wide gorge that required them to cross so they could continue on the other side. A bridge built of rope and wood slats hung across the opening betwixt the two sides. "We will need to cross." As he spoke, the wind blew, causing the bridge to sway from side to side.

Rory waited for Alana to panic. Expected her to, but to his surprise, she nodded, bravado ebbing off of her in palpable waves.

"I will cross first to confirm 'tis safe."

"What if 'tisnae? Ye will fall to yer death." Her hazel eyes rounded with the first sign of fear she'd shown since learning they would need to cross.

"I willnae. I have crossed this bridge ofttimes. Some time has passed since the last time but it still appears sturdy. First, we need to ensure ye are ready to cross after me."

She gazed at the bridge and then back to him as she worried her lip betwixt her teeth, but nodded.

"First, ye need to tie yer skirts. Ye dinnae need them to get caught in the ropes and cause issues. They will only trip ye up and that could be disaster. We dinnae want that."

With shaking hands, Alana began tying her skirts as he said and listened intently as he gave her instructions on how to cross the bridge. Where to place her feet and where to hold on to.

"Ready?" He held her hands in his as he asked, a mistake because the gesture felt all too natural. The urge to pull her into his arms and claim her mouth with his was strong. He straightened and pushed his errant thoughts to the back of his mind. It took all his strength to pull away and approach the bridge but he did so. "Watch where my feet and hands are. Once I am on the other side, just mimic what I did and we will be on our way."

She nodded and he turned to step on to the first board of the bridge.

"Rory," she called out. "Be careful," she said when he paused, his back stiff with tension.

He dipped his head and started to cross. The bridge had looked sturdy enough when he had surveyed it earlier and now that he was on it, he didn't see any structural issues. Alana should have no issue crossing as long as she followed what he had told her. He looked over his shoulder and saw that she was watching him closely, albeit whilst she was wringing her hands together.

Good.

That was exactly what he wanted her doing. Not wringing her hands together and fashing, but paying attention to his movements. His foot and hand placements.

He crossed easily and when he stepped onto the other side, he turned and called out to Alana. "'Tis yer turn now."

She approached the bridge, her shoulders straight. No panic. Her brows furrowed with determination.

"Nice and easy. Just like I showed ye."

Nodding, she took the first step, tentative at first, but with each following step, her confidence bloomed. Her steps became steadier and more sure-footed.

"Ye are doing great, lass," he urged, providing words of support to spur her on the rest of the way. As she neared the midpoint, he called out, "Ye're halfway thr—."

The board under her right foot snapped, loosening from the rope of the bridge, and crashed to the rocks below. "Alana!" Rory yelled, his heart lurching, but Alana kept her composure, took a deep breath, and continued to cross. She didn't scream. She didn't cry. In that moment she was stronger than him.

Rory's heart raced with each step she took that brought her closer to him. He wanted to tell her to hurry, but was afraid if she hurried her pace, she would slip. Instead, he watched her intently, sending a silent prayer to the lord above for her safe crossing.

Stepping from the last board, she jumped onto solid ground and into Rory's waiting arms, a huge smile stuck on his face, a triumphant look on hers. He steadied her and their eyes locked. Both of them breathing hard. Their chests rising and falling against each other's.

"I didnae think ye could do it," he muttered, burying his nose in her hair, losing himself for a brief moment, forgetting his earlier vow to not succumb to his feelings.

"I didnae either," she admitted, burrowing her face in his chest.

He wanted to stay in this position forever. Pride flickered in him at her strength. She was stronger than he had given her credit for and he found that realization annoying. His underestimation of her capability was shameful. It said far more about him than it did her. And he realized he was guilty of treating her in much the same way her family had. Not seeing her as enough.

When she was far more than enough.

Coughing, he broke contact and stepped away, tamping down the emotions that had begun to consume him once again. He kenned better. The more feelings that he allowed to surface, the angrier it made him. Alana Duran could never be his. He would be wise to remember that.

He tried to brush off how perfect she felt in his arms. "We

need to get moving," he snapped, not willing to delve into what he was feeling right now. It would do him no good. "We've got a lot of ground to cover today," he said gruffly.

Alana fell into step beside him, walking with the confidence of a thousand warriors. He remembered her feet and the blisters that had formed. It had been a few days and they'd mostly healed, but he couldn't ignore how she hadn't complained. Not once. Even when she had every right to.

As they walked on, he couldn't help stealing glances at her. His gaze lingering longer than it should. Longer than was proper. He watched the surety of her steps. The square of her shoulders. The stubborn jut of her chin.

He was impressed at her tenacity. Moreso than he would ever admit.

CHAPTER TEN

After another day of traipsing through the beauty of the Highlands, they made camp near a quiet lake. Tension still hung heavy in the air betwixt them. A remnant from whatever had passed betwixt them earlier.

For a moment, after she'd crossed the bridge and landed straight into Rory's strong arms, she had dared to dream that Rory was her betrothed. But, he had quickly squashed that when he had realized what he was doing.

But she had noticed the way he held her with all the care of a fragile being. The way he nuzzled her hair. Those weren't actions of someone who cared naught for her. Nay, those were actions of someone who cared greatly for the person they were embracing.

She'd reveled in those brief seconds. Burning the feeling into her memory so she would have it to latch on to when she was given over to her true betrothed. Wrong as that may be.

Alana may not ken much, but she didn't have to think very hard to ken that her husband-to-be would never hold her so gingerly.

And that made her angry. Why could she not be given the chance to love and be loved? She walked to the shore of the lake and sat down on the pebbly sand, looking out over the dark blue water, so different from the water at the Falls of Fae they had climbed to. A gentle wind blew, causing slight ripples to run across the surface afore gently lapping the shore. On the surface, the clouds reflected on the lake, slowly moving away from her to the other side. She wished she could escape her predicament like the clouds could escape their reflection. If she could, she would run far, far away. Where she couldn't be found, and no one would ken her name.

Lost in thought, she didn't hear Rory approach and pick up a pebble. She watched as he skipped it across the surface. It made four hops afore it sank into the dark blue depths.

He looked at her but remained silent. Waiting.

She sighed. She didn't like the blanket of tension that had been hovering over them all afternoon. Looking up at him, she squinted. "Will ye sit with me?" She asked quietly.

He pondered her question for a long moment, his lips pressed into a thin line afore finally nodding. Dropping down beside her he bent his right leg at the knee and rested his arm on it as he looked out at the water, avoiding her gaze, and waited.

Taking a deep breath, she decided to let him in. To see the person that she was inside. Not the one he thought he kenned when he'd been sent to escort her to her new home.

"Less than two months ago, I found out aboot my betrothal," she began. "The news took me completely unawares as I hadnae seen it coming. Nor did I expect it. I was told 'twas time I performed my duty for my family. For our clan. My father had sought an alliance to secure the safety of the Duran clan. We are one of the smaller clans and with the English to the South and larger clans surrounding us, we needed protection. An alliance to a strong clan that once 'twas announced we had joined forces, the constant attacks of our land would stop. The price for that alliance was my hand."

Rory scoffed and shook his head. "Ye've lived in a gilded cage all this time. I am sure yer new husband will provide ye the same type of life ye are accustomed to."

Alana bristled, not liking his accusatory tone. "Ye are naive if that is what ye believe."

"I would ne'er marry for obligation. I dinnae care who ordered me to do so."

"Ye say that, but ye cannae really ken until ye are put into the position. Look at how yer father ordered ye to escort me. Ye listened to him then. Ye obeyed his order."

He tossed another rock into the water. It entered with a plop and a small splash. "'Tis different. He wasnae ordering me to marry ye." He started to say something else, but snapped his mouth shut.

"No' e'eryone has the luxury of choice in such matters. Some of us must do what is demanded of us—no matter how unpleasant it may appear to be. I had no such choice of refusal. Growing up as a young lass, I had been told ad nauseam aboot what my duty to my family was. I kenned that I would eventually be used as a bargaining tool."

Rory scoffed. "So ye are the one responsible for the chains ye now find yerself in. Yer own complicity is to blame for yer betrothal."

Alana frowned. Had the man not listened to a word she had said? That was not what she had explained at all. "I didnae say that."

"It sounds to me like ye did. Ye kenned yer whole life that this would be yer fate. If it was something ye were so against, ye would have found a way to extricate yerself from yer predicament."

She laughed. She couldn't help it. "Ye are daft if that is what ye truly believe. I had no choice. My father made it quite clear of that. As did my mother."

Rory shook his head. "Nay, ye always have a choice."

"Mayhap ye do!" She couldn't keep the shrill from her voice, but the man was so frustrating. She threw her hands up in the air. "'Tis different for men, ye weel ken that. Women rarely have a say in such matters. *I*," she jabbed her thumb at her chest. "Did no' have any say. I was given no other option. I was *ordered* that this would be my future. I couldnae say nay." She swiped at a tear that threatened to spill over onto her cheek. She wasn't crying because she was sad. She was crying because she was mad. It was a trait that had always been seen as a weakness. But her angry tears made her stronger. Made her sit up straighter. Push back her shoulders and jut her chin out stubbornly. She felt that Rory was attacking her personally and she took affront to that.

"How are ye any better than me, pray tell?" she asked.

His head snapped to hers and their eyes clashed in fury.

"Pardon?"

"Aye. Ye may not e'er be forced to marry like I have, but ye dinnae handle yer home life any better."

"Ye dinnae ken what ye are talking aboot," he snapped.

She stood and crossed her arms as she looked down at him. "Och, aye, I do. Whereas I accept my fate, kenning I can do naught aboot it, ye run away from yers. Ye spend days upon days frolicking through the Highlands. Running. Hiding away."

"I have ne'er run away from a challenge in my life," he growled.

"Nay?" She countered. "I beg to differ. Ye run all the time. And mayhap ye are not running from a challenge. Or an order. Mayhap ye run because ye are afraid to be needed."

Rory stood up so quickly that Alana stumbled back a few steps. The fury on his face had turned his usually bright green eyes to the color of the darkest moss on the moors. His fists clenched at his sides, he stood there for a few minutes, his eyes boring into hers.

She wanted to shrink under his gaze, but she refused to show him weakness and matched his intense gaze.

Without a word, he stormed off to gather firewood, leaving her alone.

Fighting tears, Alana ran back to where they'd set up camp and rummaged through her pack for the amber fossil her mother had given her. Clasping it to her chest, she sank onto her blanket and cried silently as she stroked the cool stone.

Rory didn't understand her predicament. He thought that she

could just say no to her father's orders and that would be the end of it. How little he kenned about a woman's place in the world they lived in. He saw everything through a man's eyes. Life would be so much easier for her if she was afforded that luxury. But she was not.

She couldn't refuse the betrothal. She could only hope that it would be somewhat pleasant.

Why couldn't Rory see that she didn't have a choice?

CHAPTER ELEVEN

RORY GRUNTED AS he chopped a piece of wood with more force than he needed to. Alana's words replaying in his head. She had gotten under his skin when she said he ran because he was afraid to be needed. Her remark hit close to his heart.

Too close.

And it irked him.

How could this woman, who he had kenned for less than a sennight, how could she ken him better than his own family?

The thought that the walls he had erected were standing tall and strong crumbled. Just like his walls when it came to Alana.

He split another piece of wood with a fierce blow. It felt good to let out his frustration, but the physical exertion of his task couldn't draw out the words constantly sounding over and over in his head. Alana was wrong about one thing, though. He wasn't scared to be needed.

In fact, the opposite was true. He wanted to be needed. His second-son position in the family had set his destiny the moment he was born. He wasn't needed. He wouldn't be unless something happened to his father that prevented him from leading their clan. And even then, he still wouldn't be needed. Alpin would step in as leader, and Rory would do what he always did—leave for the comfort and tranquility of nature.

Sometimes, he allowed himself to think about what it would

be like to be needed, but not often. It was a waste of time ruminating on such trivial things.

"Shite!" He cursed to no one in particular since he was the only one in this area. He bent and picked up the kindling he'd chopped and returned to camp. Near the fire, he threw the kindling down, avoiding Alana's gaze that he could feel boring into his back.

Placing a few pieces of the kindling onto the flame, the fire crackled violently, sending hot sparks floating into the air.

Lowering himself onto the ground, he stretched his legs out and leaned back, his weight on his palms. Focused on the fire, he spoke. "I am no' scared to be needed. Naught could be further than the truth." His gaze clashed with hers for a flash of a second afore settling back on the fire. "I verra much wish to be needed." He held his hand up when Alana began to speak. "Needed for something other than escorting ladies to their betrothed."

Alana dipped her head, but not afore he saw the blush tinging her cheeks pink.

"And I am no' against marriage. I have seen many happy unions in my lifetime—my parents', my sister. They both have happy marriages. My older brother is soon to be wed and he has ne'er been happier than the times he spends with his betrothed." He sat up, resting his arm on his bent knee. "What I am against is the obligation. I dinnae want to feel obligated to marry my wife. I want to do so because of genuine feelings that stop me thinking aboot aught else."

"I dinnae think there is aught wrong with feeling that way," Alana agreed. "I would say that most people would much rather marry for love than duty."

He nodded. "Ye may no' believe it, but I have had offers. Multiple. Some werenae serious. Some were strategic. Some were genuine, at least on the lass's part," he added with a small smile. "But none of those offers interested me and I turned them down."

Alana frowned. "Yer family didnae insist?"

He shook his head. "I believe they kenned I would deny the requests when they arrived. So 'twas no surprise to them." He pulled on the back of his neck. "My family kens me weel. They oft joke that I will die alone in the mountains with only a sheep keeping me company."

Alana laughed softly, the sound a beautiful melody to his ears. "I dinnae believe that for a minute."

Her reaction surprised him. Did she not think the same of him? He felt another stone fall from the walls he'd built to protect himself.

"Do ye want to marry yer betrothed? I am no' speaking of will ye marry him. Or of duty or obligation." He tapped his fingers on his heart. "Here. I only speak of yer heart. Do ye *want* to marry that man?"

For a long moment, Alana hesitated, fidgeting with the hem of her skirts, rolling them, and then unrolling them. "It doesnae matter if I do or no'," she said finally, the tinge of sad resignation lacing her voice.

"Mayhap it should," he countered.

Their gazes met and held for a long time. Neither of them saying a word. Each of them searching the other for some unkenned answer they sought. The silence stretched long and heavy betwixt them, until Alana pulled her eyes from his.

"We should sleep now. I am for certs that the morrow will hold another long day of hiking and we need our rest."

Across the fire, she snuggled into her blanket and Rory had the sudden urge to be the one wrapped around Alana, offering her warmth from the chill of the night. Instead, kenning he was dreaming of the impossible, he laid back and rested his head on his hands as he looked up into the night sky, brilliant with thousands of stars staring back at them. They twinkled against the dark backdrop of the midnight sky. In the distance the hoot of an owl sounded, followed by another. Mates probably, Rory assessed. His gaze swept to the sky again.

What would it be like to be star? Every night they rose in the sky and were able to look down upon everyone and everything. To see what they were doing. Every night the stars rose in the same spot as if they were held there by an invisible tether, holding them in place so they couldn't escape. Or mayhap they didn't want to escape and saw their tether as an anchor, holding them in the exact spot they wanted to stay.

He sighed and stole a glance at Alana across the other side of the fire. She had fallen asleep lying on her side, her hands tucked underneath her chin.

He thought about the MacDonell. The bastard was a fool and had no idea how lucky he was to have such a beauty as Alana for his wife. He was undeserving. A burning sensation formed in Rory's chest. He rubbed at the unfamiliar feeling and then scoffed when he realized what it was that ailed him.

Jealousy.

He was jealous of the MacDonell. If their situation were different, he could see himself asking for Alana's hand in marriage. She had a smart mind. Was an excellent shot with a bow. She had a sharp tongue and wasn't afraid to say what she was thinking. She held her ground and had a deep sense of duty and loyalty to her family. That part Rory could not understand. It was her family that put her in this situation. And for what? Status? Wealth?

He would never demand such things from her. Or a daughter if he was ever lucky enough to be blessed with one. He would not force her into a marriage that would for certs make her miserable. No one wants to live their life feeling trapped.

It was why he never stayed home. Why he was always out.

But for the first time in his life, Rory thought he might like to be a star—anchored to the same spot and building a life of his own there with someone he could love and cherish.

Someone like Alana.

He fell asleep then, his mind filled with dreams of the bonny lass sleeping so close, but yet so far from him. They were running through a meadow, Alana with a braided wreath of flowers in her hair as she giggled whilst running ahead of him, daring him to catch her. When he did, he whirled her around, making her squeal, afore he captured her mouth with his.

He startled awake, reaching for Alana only to realize where he was, and that it had only been a dream. He groaned and covered his eyes with his forearm.

The world had a funny way of moving sometimes. Of course, the first time the vestiges of settling fell upon him, it was with a lass that was promised to another.

$$\longleftrightarrow \quad\longleftrightarrow$$

CHAPTER TWELVE

ALANA WALKED SILENTLY beside Rory as they navigated over fallen limbs and slippery rocks. Always there with a hand at her elbow to steady her, or an encouraging word telling her she could do something, she was finding Rory's presence to be more and more welcome.

The past couple of nights she had spent with him had given her a deeper insight into the man Rory Hart was. He was frustrating at times, but he had opened up to her as well. Sometimes she thought he fashed on whether he had said too much. But he hadn't. She had enjoyed seeing the side of him that she kenned he rarely revealed to anyone.

It made her feel special that she was the one he chose to let his guard down with. And bit by bit, she was doing the same with him. Though she still hadn't admitted that she didn't want to marry the man her father was telling her she had to. She wanted to be selfish and for once not do as she was told. To not fulfill her duty.

But she had not. She could not.

Just the thought felt like a betrayal to her family, and she couldn't do that to them. Her family's livelihood was dependent on her going through with this union.

It mattered naught how fetching she found Rory. How she let her eyes linger on him when he didn't ken she was watching.

The time spent outdoors hiking was evident in his strong build. His wide shoulders that he used to pull himself up ledges. Into trees. His arms that bulged with thick muscle honed from those same activities and more. Things like chopping wood or swimming. It was the swimming that gave him the narrow, tapered waist that she had seen glimpses of.

She sighed.

"Are ye tired?" Rory asked beside her.

"Pardon?" It took a moment for her to realize that she had sighed aloud, drawing his attention. She flushed, embarrassment washing over her. "Nay. I am fine to carry on."

He gave her an odd look but shrugged and kept moving forward. They approached a narrow trail and just afore they got there, three terrifying looking men emerged from the trees, blocking their path.

"Give us yer coin," the taller man demanded, an evil grin showing rotten teeth and Alana gasped, shrinking back in fear at the dagger the man swung in their direction.

Rory immediately pushed Alana behind him, stepping in front of her, offering her protection as his hand moved to his dirk, his back straight.

One of the thieves lunged, but he was no match for Rory. He quickly took him down with brutal efficiency, jabbing his dirk into the man's neck. Alana's hands flew to her mouth, stifling the scream that threatened to burst from her mouth. The man slumped to the ground with a soft thud and Rory quickly snatched the sword that the thief dropped.

One of the other thieves charged them, his sword raised above his head. As he swung down, Rory pushed Alana out of harm's way and countered the strike.

Strong arms circled around her waist, dragging her away from the battling men. Refusing to be taken wherever he was pulling her to, she slammed her foot onto his with as much might as she could muster. The move wasn't enough to hurt him but surprised him enough so that he let go of her. Quickly, she turned and brought her knee up, connecting with his groin. He howled in agony, but managed to reach out and grab hold of her hair as he doubled over. Wincing against the bite of pain, she maneuvered and clamped her teeth down on the man's wrist.

"Ye bitch!" He bit out through clenched teeth as he cupped his groin.

The noise distracted Rory, giving his attacker the opportunity to connect to his shoulder. Rory hissed, but brought his sword up and they continued sparring back and forth.

Before her attacker could regain his composure, Alana needed to stop his onslaught. Looking around, she noticed a rock and closed her fingers around it. Turning, she swung her arm with all her might, slamming it into the man's head. His eyes rolled back and he crumpled to the ground.

Rory made quick work of finishing the third thief off.

Alana looked around, frightened that more men would come filtering out of the trees and continue the attack. Her breaths were coming in fast, the rise and fall of her chest a rapid tempo. Tears sprouted in her eyes at the realization of the dire situation they had just faced. Her hands shaking, her eyes sought Rory's and they met his wild-eyed gaze. She noticed that he was breathing just as hard as she was.

"Ye could have been killed!" Rory growled at her.

"So could ye!" She snapped back.

"I had the situation handled." He pushed his hands through his hair and Alana saw the cut on his shoulder through the rip in his tunic.

"Ye're bleeding," she said, approaching him and gently pushed the torn material to the side so she could see.

His gaze dropped to his shoulder and he shrugged. "'Tis naught. I have had much worse."

"Mayhap so, but it needs bandaging."

He placed his finger and thumb on her chin and turned her head to the side, his brows drawing down in a frown. "Ye bleed as weel."

She brought her hand up to her cheek and when she looked at it, red shaded her fingers. She didn't remember being hit but assumed it had happened while they were scuffling.

"Come on. We need to leave." He grasped her arm and began to pull her onto the narrow path.

Pulling back, she dug her heels into the ground. "I need to bandage yer arm."

"Later. When I have ye out of harm's way."

With a quick look over her shoulder, she gave a shudder at the men lying on the ground. Two of them lay in a halo of blood, their eyes open, staring blankly at the sky.

"Dinnae look at them, lass. Ye dinnae need that memory burned into yer head."

"Are we to just leave them there?"

"Aye," Rory said, nodding curtly. "We cannae do aught for them and the one that lives will see to the bodies."

He spoke of the dead so nonchalantly and Alana realized that the sight was not foreign to him. He had seen death afore. Enough to be accustomed to it. She silently vowed to never be in that same position. Letting Rory lead her away, they walked for some distance until he deemed them safe and made camp.

"Afore ye do aught further, please let me tend to yer arm, Rory," she begged. The cut had not stopped oozing blood and if it went on much longer she feared he would drain himself.

Rory sighed, but reluctantly sank to the ground. Alana rummaged in her sack and came away with a clean shift. Using her teeth to start the tear, she pulled some of the material apart into strips. She ripped another larger piece off and dipped it into the water he had gathered at the burn they had stopped near.

Moving to clean his wound, she paused.

"Why do ye look at me so?"

She pulled her bottom lip in betwixt her teeth. "I," she started, and then paused again. She was acting foolish. Squaring her shoulders, she replied, "Ye will need to remove yer tunic if I am to clean and treat yer wound properly."

He lifted a brow. "If ye wanted to see me naked, lass, ye need only ask," he jested.

Alana felt her face flame. First from embarrassment, then, as she took in his muscled chest with just a dusting of hair, his rippled abdomen, and tapered waist, she felt herself redden even more.

"Do ye approve?" His eyes bore into hers, the corners of his mouth lifting in a small smile.

"I believe I have asked ye no' to call me lass," she said in an attempt to change the subject, even though her eyes wanted to continue to wander over Rory's exposed skin.

Focus, she thought. Wound. Cut. Clean. She finally remembered what she was supposed to be doing and moved to Rory's side.

"Surely we are much too acquainted now for me to call ye Lady Alana or Miss Duran."

Lass felt too personal. As if they had kenned each other for a long time. That was not the case, so she didn't think it proper.

"Shall I call ye by a nickname?"

She touched the wet cloth to the slice in his arms and began to slowly wipe away the bits of dried blood and stop the flow of the blood that still ran from the wound. "I dinnae have a nickname."

"Nay? Now, ye jest."

Alana shook her head. "My family doesnae believe in nicknames. One should always be addressed as their given name. 'Twas what my mother has always said."

Rory chuckled. "Seems silly to me. There is naught wrong with a friendly pet name."

"A pet name?" She asked. "Is that how ye see me?"

"No' a pet in the sense ye are thinking. I dinnae think of ye as a hound or a bird or a cat. A pet in the sense of a caring friendship."

Having cleared the caked blood away, Alana added pressure to the wound to see if she could finally staunch the bleeding.

"Caring friendship. Is that what we have?"

His gaze slid to hers, his green eyes dark. "Aye," he said and there was no deception in his tone.

"Hold this," she ordered, gesturing to the cloth on his arm. "Apply heavy pressure," she added and gathered the linen strips and another large piece of cloth. "Say that we are as ye say." She met his eyes, but quickly looked away from the intensity in which he watched her. "What would ye call me?"

Rory cocked his head to the side.

Once again she felt her cheeks flush under his scrutiny. "Ye dinnae need to answer that," she said quickly. "'Twas a daft question." She pushed his hand away. Lifting the wet cloth, she was happy to see that the bleeding had mostly stopped and applied the dry cloth afore beginning to tie the strips around it to hold it in place.

"Nay. Ye cannae back out of a question like that once asked. Hmmm. What nickname shall I give ye?" He made a show of tapping his index finger on his chin as if deep in thought. "I could call ye Little Mouse, but ye arenae meek, so that wouldnae fit. Icicle, but nay, ye arenae cold and frigid."

"Ye jest," she remarked when he could not hold his chuckle back any longer.

"Aye." He captured a lock of her hair and twirled it around his fingers. "I shall call ye Bluebell."

Alana was taken aback at that. "The flower?"

"Aye. 'Tis vibrant and colorful. Bold and beautiful and has a way of spreading its joy across the land."

She was speechless. No one had ever said aught as kind to her as that. "Ye must see me different than anyone else I have kenned. They would ne'er say such things aboot me."

"Then they are fools." He tugged her hand and she fell against him. He tucked her hair behind her ear and let his fingers slowly trail down her cheek. "Or blind to no' see it. Mayhap they are both." He nodded. "Aye. They are blind fools to no' see ye as ye should be seen."

Their faces were so close. Their mouths only inches apart. What would it feel like to kiss him? Wicked thoughts swirled through her mind. Would he kiss her? Did she want him to? She searched his face. His deep green eyes that looked at her right now as if she meant e'erything to him. A warmth swirled in her belly, coursing through her blood, making parts of her awaken. Parts that she didn't ken needed to be awakened. Instinctively, she leaned closer to him, her lips slightly parted.

His gaze dropped from her eyes to her lips and then back to her eyes again. She wanted to plead with him to kiss her. To offer her this one boon.

But she didn't have to plead. Strong arms encircled her waist, bringing her even closer to him. His mouth crashed onto hers. She gasped in surprise for a brief moment, but then gave into the temptation of Rory's lips. The wickedness of his tongue as he ran it along the seam of her lips, pushing gently for entry. She acquiesced with a sigh and then a moan escaped as his tongue invaded her mouth.

His large hands rubbed her back, then moved to her waist, then lower until they cupped her bottom and he maneuvered her so she straddled his lap.

She pushed her hands through his hair, scraping her nails against his scalp afore grasping his shoulders when he broke the kiss and moved his lips to her neck, peppering her with kisses along the sensitive skin, then her jawline, then down to her collarbone. It was too much and not enough all at the same time.

Her breaths came in short bursts as she gulped for air. "Rory," she whispered.

Suddenly, he stiffened, his lips stilling against the column of her neck. He lifted her from his lap and sat her on the ground next to him. "My apologies. I shouldnae have taken such liberties with ye." He stood awkwardly and walked stiffly away.

What had happened? She did not ken. Other than she wanted to feel his lips upon hers again. She picked up her blanket and moved it over near his. This night she did not want to sleep on opposite sides of the fire. When he returned, he looked at the blankets.

"We shouldnae."

Two words. That was all he said. Leaving the obvious unsaid betwixt them. She kenned why. But if she was going to be married to someone that could be a monster. Or old enough to be her grandfather. Nay. She would like pleasant memories to think on to get her through her days, but even moreso her nights.

Realizing she wasn't going to move, he dropped down beside her, lying on his back. She settled beside him, not touching him, but close enough to feel the warmth of his body.

He brought the plaid over to cover her and in a voice just above a whisper, he said, "Sleep weel, Bluebell."

She remained silent and smiled, liking the way he spoke the nickname he gave her and happy that he allowed her to sleep beside him without complaint.

$$\longleftarrow\!\!\bullet\!\longrightarrow\!\!\bullet\!\!\longrightarrow$$

CHAPTER THIRTEEN

THE NEXT DAY Rory lead Alana higher into the mountains. Here the paths were steeper, more slippery, and treacherous, making their footing loose. Their chances of sliding and falling were higher than when they were lower and on more stable ground. The air was colder up here. Not so cold that they could see their breaths in the air, but they would be able to soon.

As they'd hiked today, he kept thinking about the night afore. He had overstepped his boundaries. That Alana had let him surprised him more than aught. That she had enjoyed it and appeared to want more? Well, that was a dream come true. And a dream he had not had ever afore.

With her sleeping beside him last night, he had barely got any sleep himself. He was too aware of her closeness. How easy it would have been to pull her into his arms and bury his face in her neck. Her breasts. Her sweetness that he kenned would be naught less than divine.

He let out an exasperated breath. He needed to change the trajectory of his thoughts. Thinking of Alana in those ways made his walking most uncomfortable. As discreetly as he could, he adjusted himself and continued to move toward the man that would take her away from him.

And that irked him.

It should not. Alana was not his.

But she could be.

His thoughts were dangerous.

Alana kept pace with him the whole day. "This journey is taking so long, I think ye are leading me astray to spend more time with me."

His gaze snapped to hers. He wasn't prolonging their journey. But had she read him so easily? He relaxed when he saw her eyes dancing with mirth. "Ye jest," he accused.

"I do. 'Tis no' so fun when 'tis ye that is the target, is it?"

"Ye have me on that one."

"But, really, this obsession ye have with the Highlands really takes control over ye. Ye should find something else to occupy yer time." She teased again and he found himself laughing. Laughing. He couldn't remember the last time he had laughed so freely with a lass, but her humor had caught him off guard. And he found that he quite liked it.

He closed his eyes. He would groan if it wouldn't catch her attention. None of this, whatever this was, could ever come to fruition.

"Can we stop for a brief respite?" She asked.

Rory nodded, finding happiness that she felt comfortable enough with him now to ask him. Afore she would just move forward stubbornly. The dynamic betwixt them was evolving and he didn't ken how he could stop it. He didn't feel like he could. He wasn't sure he wanted to.

They sat on a large rock, the high sun offering only a sliver of warmth. Alana was wrapped in her cloak and had it tied tight around her neck. He passed her the skin of water and watched her drink. Watched the column of her neck as she swallowed.

He sucked his teeth and dragged his gaze away. Shite. One kiss and he was like a lovesick dolt. His brother would rib him endlessly if he witnessed what was happening betwixt he and Alana right now.

Alana sat with her brow furrowed, a sad look on her bonny face.

"What has ye so down, Bluebell?"

She turned her face to the sun, closing her eyes. "I find myself thinking of whate'er 'tis that waits for me when I arrive at my destination."

"At Caer Rannoch?"

"Is that where we go?"

It was Rory's turn to frown. "Aye, of course. Did the Mac-Donell no' tell ye the name of his home?"

"The MacDonell? That is to whom I am to be wed?"

Rory couldn't help his confusion at the words Alana spoke. He turned to her. "Bluebell, did yer da no' tell ye aught aboot who ye were being sent to marry?"

She shook her head.

"Have ye ever met the man?"

"Nay. Ne'er. I dinna ken who he is. Where he lives, other than north from my ancestral home. For reasons unkenned to me, my father kept all that information to himself." She drew her legs up on the rock and wrapped her arms around them, resting her chin on her knees. "I have had nightmares aboot the man I am to marry. Seeing him as an old man. Old enough to be my grandfather. Or a cruel man. I could only hope and pray that he was somewhat pleasant on the eyes and would treat me with kindness. I dinnae require much. Just kindness."

Anger simmered just under the surface of Rory's skin. How could her father keep such important information from her? Especially when he must have kenned that she would fash about what her future held. "Bastard," Rory murmured.

"Why do ye say such a thing?"

"How could yer da leave ye in the dark aboot such things?" He shook his head. "To send ye off to marry with no information is cruel."

Beside him, Alana bristled. "My father isnae a cruel man."

Rory grunted. "Indeed he is to have done such a disservice to ye. 'Tis no' right. And he had to have weel-kenned it when he sent ye to meet yer husband-to-be." He pulled on the back of his neck. "'Tis why ye ne'er say his name. Only referring to him as yer betrothed or yer husband-to-be. Because ye ken naught of the man, including his name." Rory tried to keep his disgust in check.

"What am I supposed to do?" She cried, throwing her hands up in the air. "I have told ye o'er and o'er again that I have no choice o'er the decisions that have been made for my life." She jabbed a finger into her chest. "*My* life! 'Tis no' my own to live as I please. I am just a pawn. What did it matter if I kenned his name or no'? 'Twouldnae change my circumstances."

Suddenly, Rory felt like an arse. How many times had he lamented about how he felt forgotten? As if he were an afterthought. How oft had he shirked the responsibility his da tried to place on his shoulders? Which, when he thought about it, was hardly any responsibility at all. The important things were carried on Alpin's shoulders. The demands Arthur had given to Rory, which were far and few betwixt, were naught in terms of importance when held up to Alpin's orders. It was why it upset him so much. Just as he had confessed to Alana days ago. He wanted to be needed. Truly needed. And when his father gave him a simple demand, thinking he was placating him in some way, it was easy to say no. To deny doing it.

Compared to Alana, to deny was much easier for him. A man. Women weren't offered a choice. That was the way of things. He hated it. Always had. But his dislike for people being used as pawns did not stop it from happening.

"I'm sorry, Bluebell."

Alana looked away from him, swiping at the fat tears sliding down her cheeks. "Ye havenae any idea what 'tis like."

"Ye are right, I dinnae. I hold no judgement o'er yer reaction. I would be furious if I was forced in yer situation." He wrapped an arm around her shoulders and pulled her into his chest. She pulled away from him for a brief moment, but gave in, her hand fisting the material of his tunic as she sobbed against him. Gut-wrenching sobs that shook her whole body.

Each one was like a punch to Rory's gut. He remained quiet.

He didn't ken what to say. Only kenning that he wanted to offer her comfort. Something that he felt she did not receive a lot of growing up. She deserved to be cherished. She hadn't been.

The knowledge of that upset him more than it should.

He smoothed his hand down her back, holding her close as her sobs slowly subsided.

Quite some time had passed afore she finally pulled away with a sniffle, wiping at her nose. "Ye must think me a fool."

"I dinnae," he said seriously. It wasn't a lie. She was one of the strongest people he had ever kenned. He thought of his sisters, Moira, Eilidh, and Morven, and tried to imagine them and their reaction of being sent away to wed a man they didn't ken. A man whose name they hadn't been given, nor the name of his home, or where he lived. His sisters, for the most part, were all strong-willed. They would fight, more than likely they would outright refuse.

Alana was strong-willed as well. However, when it came to her duty, her strength was in her follow-through. Her agreement to do as she was told, no questions asked, because she believed that was what her clan needed. That was a will of strength that Rory was for certs he himself did not possess.

"Look at me, Bluebell." Hands on her jaw, he caressed his thumbs over her jawline. "Ye are the strongest lass I ken. Yer strength and sense of duty would put my own to shame."

She scoffed at his words. "Now ye jest me."

"Nay." He shook his head. "I would ne'er," he said seriously.

She drew in a shaky breath and blew it out slowly, meeting his gaze. "Do ye ken him? My betrothed."

Rory clenched his jaw. The bastard was so undeserving of a woman like Alana, it pained him. "Aye," he answered quietly.

"Will ye tell me aboot him?"

Did he really want to discuss Alana's future husband with her? Nay. To do so was admitting that she didn't belong to him. He kenned she didn't. That she was promised to another. But that kiss they shared yesterday. It meant something. Even with kenning that he overstepped a line he shouldn't have. The repercussions of what would happen if it was found out. But she wasn't his. No matter how much he wished it so.

He sighed. "What would ye like to ken, Bluebell?" The nickname was forever seared in his brain now. And he kenned he would never look at the flower the same way.

"Is he old?"

"Old?" He asked, surprised. That was not the first question he expected.

"I have nightmares that he is old enough to be my grandfather. I hope 'tis no' so."

He chuckled.

"Ye laugh at me?" She asked, affronted.

"Nay, no' at ye. I would ne'er do such a thing," he promised, sweeping a strand of hair behind her ear. "I saw a vision of ye walking up the path to Caer Rannoch and finding an old man waiting to welcome ye."

"I dinnae find that comical at all."

"I am sorry ye have fashed so much o'er that. Nay, he is no' old. Our ages are similar."

Her shoulders relaxed just a wee bit at learning that. "And Caer Rannoch. That is the name of his home?"

"Aye. His father passed a few years ago, making Michael MacDonell laird and owner of the familial estate."

"Is he cruel?" Alana asked this question quietly, as if she were afraid to say it out loud.

Rory thought about how to answer Alana's question. If he spoke the truth, he would for certs frighten her. If he lied, he was leading her into a situation she wouldn't be prepared for. To lie felt like a betrayal. That was something he didn't want on his conscience.

He cared too much for Alana to not warn her of what she could expect when she arrived at Caer Rannoch.

"Michael has been kenned for no' having the most e'en of tempers," he started and paused, hating that he was telling her things that she didn't want to hear.

Beside him, Alana's brows drew down, her pretty mouth pinched into a pucker as if she had just bitten a sour apple. "He is no' kind then?" She lowered her eyes, her fingers fidgeting with the hem of her skirts. Then she laughed nervously. "Of course he is no'. Why should I have expected aught less?"

"I dinnae tell ye to hurt ye."

She faced him, bringing her hand to cup his cheek, and met his eyes, a sadness in hers that had not been there afore. "I ken that. I am no' upset with ye. Actually, I am thankful that ye have been so honest and forthcoming with me. Something that I couldnae trust from my own parents, though I should have been able to."

Rory wanted to sweep Alana up in his arms and go in the opposite direction than they were heading. To take Alana far from here. To hide them both away where no one would be able to find them. He was quite proficient. They didn't need the shelter of their families to provide for them. He could do that for them both. He leaned his head into her hand and closed his eyes, savoring the feel of the soft skin of her hand against his rough beard.

"Whate'er ye want to do, Bluebell, I will do it."

Alana dropped her hand, a sad smile on her face. "If only I could take ye up on that offer."

He clasped her hands in his, bringing them to his chest. "Ye can."

"Nay, I cannae, Rory." She shook her head. "Duty to my clan overrides aught that I may feel. The safety and weel-being of my father's people mean e'erything to me. I cannae turn against them."

"E'en at the expense of yer own happiness? Ye would give up yer freedom? Yer happiness and weel-being?" Rory asked in disbelief.

"Aye," she said quietly. "I am but one person. My clansmen are in the thousands. If me sacrificing myself for their safety is what it takes, then that is what I shall do."

Rory shook his head and pushed off the rock. "Stupid woman."

Alana jumped to her feet. "How dare ye? Ye've nay right to judge me in any way, Rory Hart. We have this same conversation o'er and o'er again and I willnae have it again," she snapped, storming off.

"Stay close." She ignored him and stomped toward the trees. "Alana," he called out, his voice stern. This time she paused. "Dinnae wander far."

"Why no'? Mayhap I will meet someone or something that will put me out of my misery." She disappeared into the cover of the trees.

As much as he wanted to chase after her, he didn't. Cradling his head in his hands, he drew in a deep breath. Damn, that woman was stubborn.

And he found that he admired that about her.

He waited for quite some time afore tracking Alana down. He busied himself getting their camp ready for the night. He found her sitting by a cliff edge, her mood sad, as she stared off into the darkening night. Not saying aught, he held out his hand to her.

Alana pursed her lips, her hazel gaze drifting from his face to his outstretched hand and then back to his eyes. Silently, she accepted and let him pull her to her feet. They walked back quietly. No words to say. Back at camp, she climbed onto the blanket he'd laid out for her earlier and curled up into it on her side.

He watched her from the other side of the fire, wanting to reach out to her so badly it hurt, but kenning he couldn't.

◄━━━━━━━◆━━━━━━━►

CHAPTER FOURTEEN

ALANA HATED THE silence that had settled betwixt her and Rory. For reasons unkenned to her their arguments really bothered her. They shouldn't. He was naught to her.

It was a lie.

But one that she didn't want to admit.

He shouldn't mean aught to her. If she would use her head instead of her feelings, she'd push him away. The smart thing to do would keep him at arm's length. But it was hard. So hard to do. Even moreso now that she kenned her future husband, Michael, as she had learned from Rory, was short of temper and even shorter with kindness.

What would it mean to her or to Rory to admit that he was starting to mean something to her? Naught could be done about it. No good would come of it. Alana needed to let those feelings go. She needed to forget they existed, no matter how hard that would to be.

They broke their fast that morning on crusty bread and berries Rory had foraged. Silently, they continued on their journey and they had not spoken a word yet. The silence was driving her mad. She couldn't take it anymore and finally gave in, starting a conversation.

"What are the local customs that ye partake in up here in the Highlands?" She asked as a way to break the silence and hoped that it was a topic that Rory could speak on for a long time. She just wanted to hear his voice as he spoke about something that he loved.

He shrugged. "We have many, I suppose. The Beltane fires in the spring. Those are always a great reason to gather and celebrate. Do ye have them in the lowlands?"

She shook her head. "Mayhap others do, but we didnae celebrate Beltane at Auchenford."

He pressed his lips into a thin line. Lips that had kissed her so passionately only a couple of nights ago. Without thinking, she brought her fingers to her lips. It was wrong that she wanted to feel his lips upon hers again. But she couldn't stop the thought from constantly popping into her mind.

"I would think that the MacDonell celebrate them, but I make no promises."

Her heart sank at the mention of her future husband. She didn't want to think about him. The dread that had settled in her stomach was growing with each step closer they got to Caer Rannoch, and she only wanted to think of happy things.

"There are also lots of *ceilidhs*. Each clan will have them for whate'er reason. Though I am for certs ye have those down in the lowlands."

"Aye. I have attended a few."

"They are big affairs here. The clanfolk all gather and my ma and da make sure to host a grand meal. After e'eryone has filled their bellies with delicious food, the music starts and dancing ensues—with lots of drink, of course." He wiggled his eyebrows, the gesture immediately lightening the mood. "There is always lots of drink on those nights."

She smiled. She couldn't help it. "They sound like a grand time." She wished her parents had hosted such grandiose gatherings.

"Och, they are. Ye should—" He caught himself and didn't finish the sentence, though both of them kenned what he was going to say. If only she could. If only their circumstances were different.

"But, some of our get-togethers are for serious matters," he said, quickly changing the subject so neither of them lingered on things they had no control over.

She stepped over a fallen log, carefully maneuvering so she didn't trip. "Such as?"

"When we gather for the honor oaths. Sometimes those are somber affairs, but no' always."

"Is that when a new laird is sworn in?" Alana's father had been laird since afore she was born, so she had never had the chance to attend an oath ceremony.

"Aye. Not always. Sometimes 'tis when a clansman has turned his back on one clan to swear loyalty to another. Or when clans combine or enter into a partnership. There are many reasons."

"Have ye attended many?"

Rory shrugged. "A few. The most recent was when my younger sister married, and she and her husband were gifted a parcel of land, and he received his title."

She realized he had mentioned his sisters and brother a few times but had not really spoken about them. Alana found herself wanting to ken more about them. But not only them individually, but them as a whole family.

"Was yer sister the first of yer siblings to marry?"

He frowned. "Aye. She took us all by surprise by falling in love with our enemy."

Alana's eyebrows shot up in surprise. "Yer enemy? Really?"

He sighed. "Aye, but I must admit that her husband treats her verra weel. He loves her truly and deeply, and she the same. It just took us some time to get used to the idea of which clan he belonged to. We had spent many years sparring back and forth. But they're coming together also brought our clans together and healed some deep-set wounds from generations past."

"It sounds like it worked out weel for ye all in the end, then, aye?"

Rory nodded his head. "It did indeed. Come, this way." He left the somewhat worn path they had been following and moved deeper into the woods.

"Where are ye going?"

"'Tis just o'er here a ways." He turned and paused when he saw her hesitation. "'Tis naught to be afraid of. I promise ye, ye will love it when ye see." He wiggled his eyebrows as he had done earlier, and gave her that genuine smile of his, and she couldn't help but feel a sort of excitement about wherever it was he was leading them.

Through the trees, the land opened up into a craggy meadow. But not just any meadow. Alana looked around in awe at the stones standing afore her.

There must have been at least twelve of them, standing tall against the backdrop of the trees. She approached them, reaching out her hand to run her fingers along them.

"Take care, Bluebell. Legend has it that if ye touch the stone and ye have the power, ye will disappear."

Her eyes widened and then she pursed her lips together when he couldn't contain his chuckle any longer. "I was going to ask ye if it were the fae again, but now I ken ye jest."

"I do. Ye make it so easy," he teased, a smile softening the harsh features of his handsome face. He lifted his shoulders and held his palms up. "It could be true, I suppose, though I have ne'er seen it happen to anyone I ken. But ye can ne'er be for certs what the fae will do."

"Who really built these? And dinnae say the fae," she warned, narrowing her eyes and pointing her finger at him.

"No one kens. These stones have been here long afore we e'er walked the land. Mayhap they were formed this way."

She thought about what he'd said. The arrangement of the rocks was much too specific to have been done naturally. Nay. The rocks were placed in the order they were by man. Or the fae. She giggled. Now Rory was having her think of fae and their possibilities.

"What are ye laughing at?"

"I was only thinking aboot who could arrange the rocks in such a way. They're massive and it would take a great feat to set them so. The fae came to mind." She lifted her brow and waited for his reaction. She was not disappointed.

Rory threw his head back and laughed loudly. "See? Now we are thinking alike." He walked to the other side of the standing stones and bent to the ground. "Look at these."

Alana walked over to where he pointed. Rocks were stacked one on top of the other. The stack was nearly to her knee. "What are those?" She asked, fascinated.

"Rock cairns. A sign of remembrance for a loved one."

"Why would it be by the standing stones? Mayhap someone did get lost by going through the stones. The cairn could be the family's tribute to their long-lost loved one."

"I dinnae—" Rory stopped when he saw the smile on her face. "Och, so this time ye jest." He smiled, and his eyes danced brightly. "Ye catch on quickly." He grasped her hand, and that familiar heat radiated through her palm and up her arm at his touch. She should pull away, but she didn't.

"We need to get back on the trail." He tugged her back toward where they had entered the trees. "We will pass another sight soon. I believe ye will like it."

Rory couldn't have been more right in his statement. After walking for some time, they came upon a ruined stone kirk. The old stone was bleached white from the sun, the surface smooth from the harsh Highland weather. Alana ran her fingers along the surface.

"There were many a handfasting ceremony held here. Not so much anymore, but there used to be. Ye could pick the wildflowers from the surrounding ground. Take a ribbon or a scarf and swear yer love to one another."

Alana kept walking along the long wall of the chapel, her thoughts wandering. "Were they forced unions?"

Rory laughed and shook his head. "Nay, no' in the least.

These ceremonies were aught but forced. They were true love matches. One where they chose for themselves."

She snapped her head to Rory. "By their own choice? No one making any demands of them?"

"Completely their own choice." He came up beside her, standing so close that she could feel the heat radiating off his body, seeping into hers. "Sometimes without their family's kenning."

Her eyes lingered on his. How she wished she could make such a decision on her own. She would choose to participate in a handfasting ceremony. With someone that she loved and wanted to build a future with. Someone kind and loving that would give her many children and in turn would love those children as much as she did.

She wet her lips and watched Rory's gaze track down to her lips afore raising and meeting hers again. Was he thinking the same thing?

A falcon screeched in the distance and broke the bond that had been building betwixt them.

"Love is really a choice here?" Alana asked, bewildered.

Rory nodded. "Aye, it always has been."

She sighed, wishing that were the case within her own family.

The rest of the day's trip was uneventful, and Alana was exhausted by the time they said their good nights over the flames on opposite sides of the fire. She found she enjoyed the nights much more when they slept close together. She felt safer. Protected. Would she feel the same way sleeping beside her future husband?

It saddened her that she didn't think she would.

Dreams overtook Alana that night. Happy dreams that she didn't want to wake up from. She dreamt of a life free from the duty of her family—one where she could choose her own husband—and she had. Rory sat on the side of a heather covered knoll and watched as Alana ran barefoot through the flowers. Her hair flowing loosely behind her. Her cheeks flushed with excitement. She was free. More free than she had ever felt in all her years. She collapsed beside Rory, breathing heavily as he cupped her face with his hands and kissed her deeply, lowering her onto a flowery bed.

She woke on a sigh. Then remembered where she was and the situation she was in. She wanted to fall back asleep so she could experience her dream once again. But she could not. Just as she could not indulge her thoughts of Rory.

One thing was for certs, she was beginning to think, for the first time in her life, that her happiness was more important than her duty. Immediately, she felt guilty for harboring such thoughts. They went against everything that had been told to her about her responsibility to her family. To her clan. But she couldn't help them.

As they walked closer to the destination that would change her life forever, she studied Rory's profile. His strong jaw, his beautiful green eyes, the long lashes that fanned his cheeks with every blink. She realized she didn't want their journey to end.

Because the ending meant goodbye.

And she didn't think she would be able to say goodbye to Rory Hart.

Not now. Not ever.

━━◆━━━━━━━━━━━◆━━

CHAPTER FIFTEEN

RAIN THREATENED THE skies once they finally were back on the trail. A village was a short distance ahead. It would veer them off their journey a bit, but Rory didn't care. He'd passed the point of not wanting to delay their arrival. Now it seemed all he wanted to do was find ways to keep Alana beside him just a wee bit longer.

They would head for the village and find shelter from the impending storm. This time, he wouldn't force Alana to stay in a musty, abandoned croft. Nay, she would have the luxury of a room. A warm, comfortable bed.

Alana was curled into her cloak, her head down, practically tucked into the warm wool. But she made no complaint. Only followed him, trusting him wholeheartedly.

He wondered when the shift had come. When had he suddenly started to long for Alana to stay by his side? He wanted to tell her about his family. His brother and sisters. His parents. Hell, he wanted to tell her about Hartsmoor and his favorite place to escape the raucousness of the castle.

"Is that a village?" Alana asked in awe, pointing to the tip of a chapel that came into view as they climbed a hill.

"'Tis." He looked up at the sky just as a fat drop of rain fell and landed in his eye. He squinted and wiped it away. "I was hoping to get there afore the rain began to fall, but it appears we willnae."

Within minutes, cold rain splashed down, soaking them both to the bone. Rory was for certs the contents of their bags would also be sopping messes once they finally found shelter.

They hurried their steps, but Rory took care so that Alana didn't slip and hurt herself. In the village, he found the inn, nestled against the mountain, it was tiny and quaint, and it would be the perfect place for them to dry and enjoy a hearty meal and a good sleep.

Rory ushered Alana inside and immediately she moved to the hearth where a fire roared. Rubbing her hands together in front of it, she sighed in contentment.

He hid a smile at the joy that sigh brought him.

"We will need two rooms, please," Rory addressed the inn-keeper who held smiling blue-eyes and a shiny bald head. His shoulders were hunched over, and he walked with a slight limp as he moved to his ledger.

"I am sorry, sir. I have only one room left—with one bed." His stare slid over to Alana and then back to Rory, a frown turning down his mouth.

Rory tensed, his gaze clashing with Alana's.

Her lips were pressed into a thin line as she pondered their situation. Finally, with a shrug she sighed. "'Tis fine. It doesnae seem like we have much of a choice, do we?"

"I do apologize, sir."

Rory waved off the old man's apology. "There isnae need to apologize. We are just happy to have shelter from the storm." He nodded toward the door. "The rain came on quick and strong." The man nodded and handed Rory a key.

He paid the man the stated price and then picked up their packs and guided Alana to their room.

Inside, he set their bags on the floor as Alana stopped and assessed the room.

"There will be no wandering hands this night," she warned.

Rory put his hands up in defense. "Ye will get none from me," he promised and began unpacking their items and laying them out near the hearth so they could dry. He walked to Alana and untied her cloak, slipping it off her shoulders so he could hang it too by the fire. Because it was so wet, the wool would take the night to dry, he was for certs.

Her teeth began to chatter, and he rubbed her arms with his hands, trying to get her warm.

"Let us go downstairs. The innkeeper had mentioned that there was warm cider to be had in the main room."

She let him lead her out the door and down the hall and stairs. They went past the desk where they had secured the room and entered a large, open room. Two huge hearths were on opposite walls, their fires burning bright. Chairs were arranged in front of them, and he led Alana to one and had her sit. He pushed the chair a little closer so she could dry off and warm up.

A young servant appeared at their side. "Might I suggest the warm, spiced cider? 'Tis made special by the innkeeper's wife and will warm ye from the inside out."

"That would be lovely. Thank ye," Alana said through clattering teeth.

"We need to get ye warmed up, Bluebell. Ye will catch yer death if we dinnae."

"It would happen faster if I werenae in these dreaded skirts that are soaked through. But seeing how all of our items are wet, I will make do." She looked into the dancing flames. "At least the fire is strong. I can feel the heat seeping through my clothes, so they should begin to dry soon."

Rory nodded and sat in the chair beside her. He didn't ken what to think. If they were married, this would seem like a normal adventure. He would reach across the space betwixt them and hold her hand as he caressed his thumb over her soft skin. But seeing how he was escorting her to her future husband, their predicament was not one they should be sharing.

And he didn't even want to start to think about what the night held for them.

One bed to be shared betwixt them again. They had done so afore with success. He wasn't sure he could do so again.

The servant girl arrived with their ciders, and they thanked her as she placed them cups on the nearby table.

He was tired. Alana must be as well. It would do her good to sleep in a bed for the night. She'd spent so many nights sleeping outside, and he thought that she had earned this night of luxury. He was glad he had the ability to give it to her.

Sipping the cider, he was pleasantly surprised. He was expecting a spicy grog that would assault his tongue, but this drink was delicious and the lass was right—it did warm him from the inside.

"Do ye like it?"

Alana looked at him with a strange look on her face. "Like what?"

He lifted his mug. "The cider."

"Och, aye. 'Tis verra tasty. We should compliment the innkeeper's wife if we have the chance to meet her. I dinnae think I want to move from this spot. 'Tis quite cozy and warm." Her voice was low, dreamy. "Tell me aboot yer family, Rory," she said over the low din of the crowd and the crackling of the fire.

"What would ye like to ken?"

She shrugged, her hands wrapped around the warm cup. "Start with yer parents. That seems the natural thing to do."

He smiled. As much as he hated when his father mentioned duty to him and as much as he yearned to feel needed, he kenned he was loved. Especially by his mother, Lillias. He leaned in close to Alana. "My mother is English," he said conspiratorially.

Alana's eyes widened in surprise. "Really?"

"Aye," Rory chuckled, "though she has been in Scotland for a verra long time. Ye wouldnae really ken in a brief meeting. She adapted to Highland life quite weel."

"Was the union betwixt she and yer father arranged?"

Rory rolled that question over in his mind. "In a sense I suppose ye could say 'twas."

Alana furrowed her brows, her forehead creased in confusion.

"Ye see, my da was visiting his cousin on the borderlands. Mayhap no' far from where ye and yer family hail. Anyhap, he and his cousin went to spend the Epiphany in Midrummil."

Alana sucked in a breath, her eyes rounding.

"Are ye familiar with it."

She shook her head. "I have ne'er been, but I ken of the legend of the well."

Rory smiled. "Aye, weel, that is how my parents met. 'Twas fate, or at least that is what they tell me and my siblings all the time."

"I dinnae ken I have met anyone that the legend held true for. Of course, I dinnae travel to that town, but that is verra nice to hear that the legend is real. I would love to meet yer—" Her words dropped off afore she could finish her sentence. But Rory kenned what she was going to say. She would love to meet his parents. Hell, he'd be lying if he said he didn't want her to meet them.

"My mother would like ye verra much."

"Why do ye say such a thing?" She sipped her cider, closing her eyes as the spiced liquid warmed her.

"She just would." He laughed. "She always said that I would one day meet a lass that would tame my ways and make me want to settle down."

Alana's eyes clouded. "I hope ye do, Rory. Ye deserve naught less."

Their gazes held for a few long moments. How could he survive kenning that the woman that could do that was sitting beside him and he had no choice but to let her go. Let her go to a bastard that was so undeserving of her that it would be physically painful to offer her up to that weasel MacDonell.

The servant girl returned. "If ye would like to move to one of the dining tables we will have a meal brought out to ye," she offered kindly.

"I would rather stay by the fire to keep warm," Alana said. "Ye go ahead, Rory. I will sup later."

The girl straightened. "Ye are still wet from the rain, aye? We will move a table near so that ye may continue to dry whilst ye sup. We wouldnae want ye to catch yer death from the damp."

The girl spun on her heel and spoke with an older servant that watched near what Rory assumed was the kitchens.

"Thank ye for being so accommodating," Alana said to the servants after they'd moved a table and loaded it with trenchers and trays with foods of all assortments. The hearty meal had Rory's mouth watering when the divine scents tickled his nose.

"Ye choose what ye would like first, Bluebell."

"I dinnae think ye need to wait, Rory. There is plenty."

He nodded, and they ate, filling their bellies as if they hadn't eaten for weeks. He told Alana about his brother, Alpin, who was engaged to be married. He had already told her about Moira, but he told her about his sister, Eilidh, and how she loved to play the fiddle and how she traveled around in some musician circles playing for *ceilidhs* and such. And then his younger sister Morven, the youngest of the family. Always pushing everyone's limits and shirking out of all responsibility. He had chuckled at that, realizing he did the same thing with the small responsibilities his father tried to assign him. This one not included. Escorting Alana to her destination was aught but a small order.

Alana listened intently, paying attention to all the details of his siblings as if she were trying to memorize them.

"I had once dreamed of mapping the whole of the Highlands. Plot by plot. But I kept getting drawn back home for one thing or another."

She bumped him in the shoulder. "For things like escorting me north?"

He tilted his head as he looked at her. "Aye. But I wouldnae change it." It was the truth. He would not if given the chance. It was why he wanted to savor every minute left he had with Alana. He kenned as they drew higher into the Highlands, they drew closer to the MacDonell. Which meant closer to letting her go forever. It wasn't something he was ready to face at this moment in time.

"I had always thought my parent's loving. I was coddled as a child. But I see now that I was being sheltered. Kept away from everyone that wasnae family. I had ne'er thought aboot it. I just thought 'twas the way of it." She laughed bitterly. "Now, in my current predicament, I find myself questioning everything."

Rory listened intently as Alana spoke about her family and what her life was like as a child.

She pushed food around on her plate afore finally taking a bite of roast venison. "My clan had been near devastation after my grandfather's death. My father built it back up so we once again flourished, but the past years have been hard. Our lands have been attacked and pilfered. My brothers havenae been able to marry as they have naught to offer." She chewed her lip for a moment. "That is why my betrothal was put in place. A truce. The offer of protection from a larger clan from the surrounding clans that attack us endlessly. Protection from the English as weel." A sad smile lifted the corners of her mouth. "I only wish there was another way. But there is nay turning back now when all the pieces have been put in place." Her eyes were sad as she sipped her cider and stared into the flames of the hearth, the light reflecting in her round eyes.

Back in their room, they readied for bed, but neither of them moved to climb into it. Firelight danced over Alana's features, making her hazel eyes appear dark gray, her high cheekbones harsh and defined.

"We cannae stand here through the night. 'Twill for certs make for an exhaustive day on the morrow," Rory offered, pushing his hands through his hair.

Pressing her lips into a thin line, Alana nodded. She slipped under the throws and stayed near the edge of the bed. "Remember, no touching," she warned over her shoulder.

Rory held his hands up in defense. "I promise." Though as he slid in beside her, he fought the temptation to press his front against her back that faced him. The feel of her body in his arms would offer him the best sleep. But he promised and he would keep his word. Following her lead, he moved to his side, so his back was to hers, but sleep did not overtake him any time soon. He couldn't sleep with her so close. He laid awake for what seemed like hours afore he finally drifted off.

CHAPTER SIXTEEN

THE NEXT MORNING, Alana sat by the hearth sipping honeyed tea whilst she watched Rory chat with the innkeeper's grandchildren. They'd learned that the innkeeper's daughter and her children lived with him and helped him run the inn. Her husband had tragically perished in a fire two years afore.

Rory picked up a lad and spun him around whilst pulling a funny face and Alana nearly choked on her drink. A fit of coughs erupted and Rory looked at her with concern, but she waved him off to continue playing with the children. He hesitated, but as she dismissed him with her hand once more, he turned back to the child, crossing his eyes and sticking out his tongue.

The lad and his sister broke out in fits of laughter. Their giggles filling the room with a happiness and cheer that Alana hadn't realized she longed for. Her brothers were older than her and neither of them had any children. Auchenford Castle was usually quiet. It missed the liveliness that laddies and lassies brought with them.

"Twirl me, twirl me," the lass begged, reaching up her arms so Rory could spin her around the same way he had spun her brother. "Weeeee," she squealed, grasping at Rory's neck, and squeezing.

He stopped and set her on her wobbly feet, waiting for her world to right itself afore he let go.

109

The lad tugged on his tunic and when Rory looked at him, he pointed to his boot, which had come untied.

Quickly, Rory knelt, tying the boy's shoe, listening to him ramble on with a huge smile on his face.

The scene hit Alana like a rock had just fallen on her. The image of Rory seared into her mind. She burned the pictures in her memory. Rory as a father. Rory with a home. Rory as hers. A dream she wanted but didn't dare dream of. It would only lead to her ruin and disappointment at what her future held.

But at that moment in time, it was so easy to believe he was hers. That the children were theirs, and that the inn was their home. That they were spending a normal morn as a family.

Later, Alana helped the innkeeper's daughter, Joanna, wash the dishes. She listened intently as the woman gossiped about Rory and his family. "The Hart's are a caring and loving family. No' one of them has a bad bone in their body. But Rory," she dipped her head toward the corner where Rory sat with the children on his lap as he told them a story that had them both enraptured. That familiar tug flipping her stomach as was beginning to be commonplace when it came to thoughts of Rory.

"He is special," Joanna continued. "He has a heart for the highlands. He may look wild and untamed, but under all that wilderness is a heart of gold," she said kenningly.

"Ye ken him weel, then?" Alana asked, an unexpected jolt of jealousy ripping through her body.

"The Hart's are weel kenned e'erywhere. Rory especially so since he travels the lands so much. He is always visiting the different villages."

Alana dried the trencher that Joanna handed to her.

"I thank ye for the help. 'Twas most kind of ye."

"'Twas the least I could do," she said with a smile and she meant it. It was nice to feel useful—and not in the sense of what she could do for her clan. But in the physical sense. At home she would never had entertained the idea of washing or drying dishes. They had servants for all that. But she found the work gratifying.

"I will put together food for ye to take on the road with ye as ye continue yer journey." Joanna disappeared only to return a short time later, a bundle wrapped in linen and twine in her hands. She handed it to Alana with a hug. "This should sate ye weel as ye carry on."

"Thank ye for yer kindness."

Joanna nodded. "Remember," she whispered, a twinkle in her eye and a kenning smile on her lips. "A heart of gold."

Alana gave her a wistful smile. If only she kenned how much it couldn't be so.

"Ready?" Rory asked, hobbling over to her, the two children each clinging on to a leg.

"Come now, ye wee beasties," Joanna chided. "Let Master Rory be on his way. He has much traveling to do this day."

They grumbled but reluctantly released Rory's legs. He bent and gave them each a warm hug. The children looked so tiny enveloped in his muscled arms. "I will see ye again soon, aye?" They nodded simultaneously, each sticking out their lower lip in a pout. "Now be good for yer mama. Understand?"

"Aye, Master Rory." They answered and moved to grab their mother's skirts as Rory and Alana left the inn.

"Lady Alana!"

Alana spun to see the lad running toward her. "I forgot to give ye this." He thrust a purple flower toward her.

Smiling, she knelt and gave the boy a hug. "Thank ye. I shall treasure it fore'er."

With a toothy grin he gave her a wave and turned to run back inside the inn.

"Those wee children are adorable."

"Aye. 'Tis hard for Joanna since her husband has passed, but she seems to be doing weel with her da."

Back on the road, Rory carried both of their packs, one of them stored the food from Joanna. Her mind was wandering as they walked. Her thoughts consumed her. And the man walking beside her was the main attraction in those thoughts.

At the inn, Rory had revealed a side to him she hadn't yet seen. She found herself liking it. Very much. Whilst he wasn't as cold and standoffish now as he was when they had first met, she had never seen him let down his guard so much as he did with the children. It was as if he was a whole different person. She realized that was his true self. The person he was when he let down all the walls he had built up around him. She wished she could see that man always.

She hugged the flower close. Had Rory given the lad the idea to gift it to her? She couldn't help but wonder. But then, she also found herself wishing it to be true.

"What 'tis on yer mind, Bluebell? Ye are off in yer own wee world it seems."

"'Tis naught. Just…thank ye." She quickened her pace and moved ahead of him a bit. She could feel his eyes watching her. She kenned they were. She didn't need to see his stare to ken it was there.

He didn't call her back. He let her walk and kept the distance betwixt them. Her consuming thoughts continued, and for the first time, she wondered if she was for this world after all.

Mayhap, she was meant for the Highlands.

But with who?

CHAPTER SEVENTEEN

RORY CAUGHT HIMSELF as he watched Alana stretch in the afternoon sun, his eyes lingering longer than they should, edging the line of being improper. But he found he could not control himself. He could not stop looking at her. Watching her. Longing for her. He felt it deep in his bones.

"The birds are active today," she commented, squinting against the sun, holding a hand up to shield her eyes as she looked at the trees. Birdsong had followed them throughout the day. Rory hadn't paid it much attention. He was so used to the noise that it blended into the background of what he always expected to hear.

"Aye," he agreed. "They have much to talk aboot, apparently."

Alana smiled. A huge, bright smile that transformed her face and made him want her even more. "What must it be like?"

"Pardon?" He wasn't sure to what she was referencing.

"Dinnae ye e'er wonder what 'twould be like to be a bird? To fly freely aboot from one place to the next." She put her arms out imitating wings and flitted around in a small circle. A giggle bubbling up and bursting from her mouth.

Her laugh had become familiar. Something that he looked forward to hearing. So much so, that he kept trying to find ways to make her laugh, not caring if he was making a fool of himself.

Her presence no longer grated at him. Nay, it stopped doing that days ago. Now it comforted him. And for the brief moments she was not near, he longed for her.

He hated the warmth that bloomed in his chest every time she looked at him. It made him want to puff out his chest and square his shoulders, as if he was some buffoon preening for her attention. But no matter how he tried to stop all the feelings growing within him, no matter how he tried to tamp them down, they kept surfacing. And he was finding it hard to ignore them.

Rory sighed. "I would always be on edge. A predator could be watching from the shadows and wait for me to take off in flight so it could snatch me out of the air."

"Rory," she scolded. "That is a dreadful way to think of it."

He shrugged. "Ye asked. I am only being honest."

"Weel, I do appreciate that. E'en if 'tis morbid the way yer mind works." They paused to refill their skins at a bubbling waterfall. The spray of the water caused her hair to cling to her glowing cheeks.

He wanted to reach out and brush the hair back. To feel her soft skin under the pads of his fingers. But he didn't. He fought the urge with all his might.

When she stumbled on a slippery rock with a squeal, her feet coming out from under her, Rory grabbed her waist—holding on too tightly. Their eyes locked. The moment pulsed betwixt them. She was breathless. So was he.

Neither of them moved to pull away. Not wanting to break the spell that had bound them in that moment.

Finally, Rory stepped away, letting go, he strode ahead. Angry with himself for acting like a besotted lad.

Her brow furrowed, but he made no move to explain his mood. Instead, he pushed them forward. Forcing them to move further along in their journey than he had originally planned for the day.

By the time they had stopped for the night, both of them were exhausted and hungry. As they sat by the fire, each of them on opposite sides of the flames as they had most nights, they didn't speak.

Rory remained quiet for fear of saying something he would regret. In no way could he make her aware of the feelings that were building within him. It wouldn't be fair to her. Not when she had no choice in the matter that waited for her in the North. Nay, it would be cruel of him to say aught that would cause her to feel guilty for moving forward.

Though would she? Feel guilty that is. Mayhap it was only him having these sinful thoughts and she did not think of him in the same manner. The realization was crushing, but he would keep mum on the fact. It would be easier to let her go if her feelings didn't match his.

A few times as they supped, Alana tried initiating a conversation, but he avoided it. His head consumed by thoughts that could never come to fruition. He busied himself with sharpening his blade.

When Alana finally gave up on trying to engage him and wrapped herself in her blanket, her back to the fire and him, a pang of guilt hit him square in the gut.

He sighed. He was being an arse again, but if he wanted to get through the rest of this journey unscathed and with his heart intact, it was the way he would have to be. Once his blade was sharpened enough to slice a blade of grass in a single swoop, he tucked it away.

He wasn't tired. Sleep would escape him this night, so he moved to a nearby tree to lean against that as he stared at Alana's back. Could she feel his gaze upon her, he wondered? Had she fallen asleep, or was her mind reeling as much as his?

If she was still awake, were the reasons denying her sleep the same as his? Mayhap her mind was struggling with what the future held with her soon-to-be husband. Rory wanted to groan at the thought of MacDonell. He couldn't even think of the louse without wanting to punch something. Preferably, the dolt himself. The bastard didn't deserve Alana.

MacDonell wouldn't treasure her as she should be treasured. She should be cherished like the finest and rarest of jewels. But he wouldn't. If he was being forced into this marriage as well, he would more than likely lock her in her chambers and only visit when it was time to… He cut the thought off afore he could finish it. Nay, he didn't want to think of Alana's future so bleakly.

The man would have had to agree to the marriage. He was laird so there was no one forcing his hand. Though why he wanted to get involved in a lowland's clan, Rory couldn't figure out. It made no sense. From what Alana had said, the Duran's had naught to offer. She carried no dowry. Or at least none that he had seen or heard her mention.

She sighed heavily and Rory realized she hadn't fallen asleep.

He could go to her. Wrap his arms around her, bury his face in her neck, breathe in her sweet scent.

"Shite," he swore quietly, grinding his fist into the ground.

Instead of thinking of the things he wanted to do, he needed to remind himself of all the reasons why he couldn't fall for the bonny lass.

Stop. She is not bonny. She is just a lass.

A lass that I call Bluebell because of her beauty.

He sighed. Think, Rory, he urged himself. Remember why ye cannot have Alana Duran. Think of all the reasons why she can never be yours.

One, he ticked off on his fingers, she is promised to another.

Really, if he was truthful, that was the only reason why. It overrode all other reasons. She could not be his. No matter how much he wished it so. She belonged to MacDonell, and kenning the arse, whether the man wanted Alana or not, he would do all in his power to keep her. Whether because of the promise, or just plain spite to keep her away from Rory.

Their clans weren't mortal enemies, but they also weren't close. It was why his father pushed for Rory to step in and help Alana. It would make a show of good faith to the MacDonell, and that was always a benefit. Even if the clan was further North where they couldn't really offer any sort of protection. Which got Rory to thinking.

If MacDonell land was too far from Hart land, it was for certs more than too far to be of any benefit or assistance to the Duran. So, what then, was the real purpose for the marriage? It wasn't as if the Duran clan held many numbers. They did not. The clan was quite small and had gotten smaller over the past several years.

So, what then?

Rory pondered that question all night as sleep eluded him. When dawn finally broke he readied food and drink for Alana to break her fast. He wanted to get moving as fast as possible this morn. The trek ahead was getting more difficult the closer they got to MacDonell lands.

But he also wanted to sit here and get to ken Alana more. He shook his head. Against every fiber of his being, he could not admit to himself that he would have to let her go.

◄——————————►

CHAPTER EIGHTEEN

ALANA HAD A restless night. Though not as restless as Rory had by the look of weariness weighing his handsome features down. Dark circles shadowed underneath his tired eyes. After initially lying down with her back to Rory, she ended up tossing and turning for most of the night afore finally settling into a deep sleep when dawn was just getting ready to break.

She woke to a meal waiting for her to break her fast. She ate and hurriedly got ready. Rory had mentioned that he wanted to leave early and she would not delay them.

They had been climbing the trail and it had grown steeper and steeper with each step they took. She was in a dour mood and she could not explain why. Mayhap it had to do with the way she felt Rory had shunned her the night afore. He spurned away every attempt she had made at conversation. She could tell he was lost in his own thoughts, much like she had found herself all too often lately.

Though she wasn't sure why his thoughts would put him in such a foul mood. He was not the one being forced to marry someone that was unkind. His future wasn't bleak. Not like hers.

"Careful," he warned, breaking into her solemn thoughts.

For some reason his word of caution annoyed her. "I will be just fine," she snapped. "I think that by now, after all the days we have been hiking that ye would think me capable of continuing to do so." She rubbed her nose from the sudden itch that surfaced at the same time a stone loosened under her foot. A sharp pain shot through her ankle, like a spear of hot flame, and she yelped as she tumbled down.

Rory rushed to her, and she could tell that he was trying to catch her afore she hit the ground, but he wasn't fast enough.

At her side, he knelt and gently checked her ankle. She whimpered as his prying fingers hit a sensitive spot.

"Ye're too stubborn for yer own good," he muttered, scooping her into his arms in one swift move.

"Put me down," Alana protested, pushing at his chest, flustered. But he only snorted, ignoring her and refusing to set her on her feet. Trying to ignore the throbbing of her ankle, she rested her head against his chest. She could hear the strong thump-thump-thump of his heart, racing in tandem with hers.

He carried her to a sheltered ledge, the overhang of rock protecting them from the sun. Gently, he set her down, taking care to not cause her pain. "Please, for once, listen to me and dinnae move," he pled with her as he walked away, only to return a few minutes later with their packs.

Dropping them on the ground, he dug around and pulled out a linen tunic which he began to tear into wide strips.

She protested, but he didn't stop.

"I need to wrap yer ankle. 'Twill be swelled soon and the wrapping will help. 'Twill also help keep the pain down. 'Tis no' broken though, which is a blessing considering how hard ye fell."

He dropped down beside her and gently lifted her leg. He wrapped her ankle in the strips of linen with nimble fingers that moved light as feathers.

How he could be so big and rough, but treat her with such kindness and gentility, she hadn't the faintest idea. When he finished, he set her leg on the ground. "If ye stay off it for the rest of the day and night, ye should be able to walk on it on the morrow. 'Twill be sore, of course, but manageable."

She nodded and he pushed off the ground.

"I will set up camp and then prepare a meal. Stay there," he ordered.

Alana didn't ken where he thought she might go, but she dipped her head in acquiescence and watched him move around the area. He lit a fire first, close to the overhanging ledge they were using as shelter. He unfurled her blanket and brought it over to her.

"Ye might get chilled."

She accepted it and he walked off afore she could answer him.

Their surroundings weren't as lively as they were in previous days. The trees had lessened. There were still many, but not as many as had littered the ground as they wound their way up deeper into the Highlands. There were more grassy fields here, sloping up with rocks guarding the sides of the path they were following. Some were huge moss-covered boulders, some small. Some loose, like the one she had slipped on.

She adjusted her legs and winced at the slice of pain that shot up through her ankle and followed through to her leg. She was lucky she hadn't broken it as Rory had mentioned. She couldn't even imagine the delay that would cause. And whilst that would give her more time to spend with Rory, he would for certs be angry at the further postponement. Lord kens, they had experienced many hindrances on their journey so far. She didn't want to be the cause of yet another one.

So, on the morrow, when it was time for them to leave, she made the decision that no matter how much her ankle may hurt or throb, she would push through the pain. She'd done it with her blisters, she could do it through this as well.

With all the camp preparations done, he sat down beside her, so close, their arms touched. Neither of them made a move to pull away. The connection was something they both wanted, even though they shouldn't. She leaned against his side, the pain in her ankle beginning to dull just a wee bit as the warmth in her belly grew from being so close to Rory.

Lord above, would she ever have this same reaction when it

came to her future husband? She didn't want to think about that right now.

"Thank ye," she murmured.

She felt Rory shift and he brushed a loose strand of hair from her cheek, tucking it behind her ear. As he had afore, he let his fingers linger on her skin, and drag slowly away afore breaking the contact.

The space around them was quiet, as if nature was holding its breath the same way she was. She caught her bottom lip in her teeth, thinking about how much she enjoyed being this close to Rory. To soak in his warmth and gentle touch. To feel the rise and fall of his chest with each breath he took beside her.

The moment stretched, for what seemed like an eternity, and Alana didn't mind it one bit. They remained like that for what seemed like hours, but it couldn't have possibly been that long.

An owl hooted, his call breaking the silence of the night, severing the connection she had felt, causing Alana to jump.

Rory chuckled, the deep rumble bubbling up from his chest. "Ye scare easily, Bluebell."

"I dinnae. It just caught me unawares, is all."

His fingers played with the edge of the blanket that covered her. She watched his hands move back and forth, folding the edge, and unfolding. Over and over again. On constant repeat. A steady rhythm that he continued.

She snuggled closer to him, fashing that he might pull away. But he didn't. Instead, he draped a strong arm around her shoulders and pulled her in closer to him. Emboldened, she nestled even closer, burying her face in his chest. She could feel the hard planes of his muscles beneath her cheeks.

They were quiet for a while. Listening to nature as it woke for the night around them. Listening to each other's breaths. She listened to his heart as it beat beneath her ear, a steady, strong staccato.

It was late, the sun finally setting and disappearing. The flames of the fire the only light around them. It created shadows that danced along the rocks. If she were alone, she might be frightened of the images they created, but with Rory she was calm.

As the hours passed, they still leaned against each other. Neither of them tried to move away and break the constant contact they had been enjoying for the night.

It was as if they were right where they were supposed to be. In each other's arms. Connected in a way that only those who cared very much for each other could.

The fact that they could never really be, hurt. It hurt more than she would ever admit.

And that revelation broke Alana's heart.

✦

CHAPTER NINETEEN

T HE NEXT DAY'S travels were slow-going because of Alana's injury. Rory took care not to push her too hard or to make her feel guilty that they couldn't move at the pace he had originally planned. Her ankle was swollen and he kenned it ached, but she was putting on a brave front and hadn't said a word about how uncomfortable she was. Still, her pain was easy to see in way she clenched her jaw and sucked in her breath. In the squint of her eyes, and the pinch of her mouth.

So, as they climbed higher, he took their forward progress slow.

He looked up to the sky, frowning. The once sunny sky had become dreary with angry, gray clouds moving in quickly. "'Tis bad weather threatening. We should seek shelter."

Alana paused, looking around and holding her hands up. "Where exactly do ye suggest we go? There isnae a village in sight. No croft. No bothy. Just the land and us."

As she finished her sentence, rain started to fall. They hurried their pace, Alana crying out in pain as the rain fell so fast, so suddenly, it flooded the trail. Causing water to stream down the path forcing them to slip and slide. Fearful that Alana would fall again or hurt her ankle further, he pulled them off the trail.

He whipped his head around, squinting through the battering rain for an option. Nearby, he spotted a cave. "This way," he called over the roar of the wind and rain that was so similar to the storm that had led them to the abandoned croft Alana had so despised.

Gusts of wind whipped around them as he led Alana to the cave, hurrying as fast as he dared whilst still keeping her safe.

Ducking inside the cave, Rory looked around. He wanted to make sure that they weren't sharing it with anyone or any animal.

When he was for certs they were alone, he gathered wood for a fire. It was wet and would take a long time to dry enough but he found some dry wood under an alcove protected from the elements and grabbed that to bring back to the cave. It would be enough to start the fire and keep it going.

Alana was sitting against the cave wall when she startled him by breaking out into laughter. Loud peals of laughter that had her clutching her stomach.

He looked at her with a questioning expression on his face. Confusion furrowing his brows.

"What is it that ye find so amusing?" He asked, because he couldn't for the life of him figure out what it could be. There was naught comical about the situation they found themselves in.

"Look at us. Once again, wet from rain. This must be what, the third or fourth time we stop and are soaked through. Finding that we need to dry our clothing once again."

It hadn't occurred to him, but she was right. He tilted his head to the side and chuckled. "We do seem to have a knack for beckoning the rain gods."

"Aye." She looked around the interior of the cave. "Thank ye for finding such a spot. 'Twill for certs keep us dry until the storm passes."

"We may be dealing with the ramifications of the storm for days to come. The trail flooded so quickly that 'twill take time for the land to dry. With yer hurt ankle, we need to take extra precautions to ensure ye dinnae wound it further."

She stood gingerly and moved toward the fire, her limp making her amble uneven. Settling beside the flame, she pulled something out of her pocket and rubbed her fingers over the item.

"What have ye there?"

Alana met his gaze, a wistful smile on her face. "'Tis a gift from my mother. She gave it to me in the moments afore I left." She held it up for him to take so he could inspect it.

Heather in amber. "'Tis beautiful," he said and handed it back to her.

Rory moved to the entrance of the cave, looking outside at the rain that continued to fall in heavy sheets. He felt restless. Not wanting to talk, he paced the opening, back and forth, over and over.

When Alana looked into the fire or at her amber relic, he stole glances at her. Letting his gaze linger. She was so beautiful sitting there. He was for certs she had no idea the power she held in her gaze. Hell, she could bring him to his knees with a snap of her fingers. He would beg to do her bidding. His heart pounded with all the feelings she had awakened in him. Feelings that would remain unspoken. They had to.

But damn if every thing she did didn't affect him in some way. It mattered naught how wee whatever it was—the way she tucked her hair behind her ear, the way she hummed a quiet tune when she didn't think he could hear. Her awe at his beautiful Highlands. All of them hit him right smack in the gut.

Trying to keep his mind busy, he set to completing menial tasks. First, he sharpened his dagger and the extra he kept in his pack. He should give it to Alana so she would be able to protect herself if she ever found herself in danger.

It was a good idea. He wasn't sure why he had not thought of it earlier. Afore they left to continue on, he would gift her his favorite dagger. The one he carried on him at all times. Its silver handle was engraved with Celtic knots that formed a cross. A ruby set in the middle.

He also hoped that when she got to her future home and was

wed, she would keep the dagger and think of him whenever she looked at it. Rory bit back his bitter laugh. He was acting like a lovesick pup. With the daggers sharpened, he surveyed their packs, looking for rips and tears that he could repair. There were none since most of their journey had been on ground. It was different when he spent his time scaling the sides of mountains. He almost always tore his packs when he climbed.

Overall, the plan to keep his mind busy and off of Alana failed miserably.

Alana noticed him staring, and he looked away quickly. "I need take care of some things." He left the shelter of the cave and stood under the overhang. She would be safe in there without him for a while.

He looked up through the driving rain and blew out a breath. God, he wanted her. He kenned he had no right to, but he couldn't help it. He couldn't deny it any longer, no matter how many times he told himself he didn't. Guilt gnawed at him. Eating at his insides. Consuming him much like thoughts of her consumed his every waking moment.

"Rory," she called from inside. "Ye will get all wet out there. Come back inside."

"Dinnae tell me what I should be doing," he snapped. "I have spent many a night in the rain. 'Twillnae kill me." He spat the words out with much more force and anger than he meant and when she flinched, misery blanketed over him. And guilt.

She didn't deserve his ire.

He stepped into the rain and just stood there, feeling the drops soak into his tunic. The cold rain chilling his skin as it rolled down his back. But he didn't care. He needed something to cool the insatiable heat that overtook his body when his thoughts of Alana ran rampant.

How much time he spent outside, Rory didn't ken. The rain had finally slowed and his body racked with shivers, but he still made no move to enter the cave again. He'd found a fallen log to sit upon and that's what he had done for the past few hours. The night sky was black as velvet now. The heavy clouds blocking all signs of the moon and stars. It was as if he were locked in stone room with no windows. The only light offering any solace was the sliver of firelight that escaped from the entrance of the cave in the distance.

Had Alana fallen asleep yet? He hoped she had. He wouldn't sleep again this night, and if he was going to lay awake, he didn't want to have to try to keep up small talk with her. Though he needed to apologize for his earlier harsh reaction. He had no right to take his anger out on her.

Finally, he made his way back inside the shelter of the cave. Creeping along quietly, he dared a peek at Alana. She was curled up on her side, hands tucked under her cheek as she slept. She looked so peaceful. So beautiful. What would it be like to wake up to that vision every morn? He longed to find out, even though he shouldn't.

He stripped out of his soaked clothing and laid them out to dry after changing into a fresh set of clothes. Lying on his blanket, he stared through the flames at Alana's silhouette. All he wanted to do was lie next to her and soak in her warmth. To let her heat his skin. To set him aflame.

The distance betwixt them was like a curse. It hurt to be so close and not be able to touch her. But without the distance, his resolve would slip. He could feel it slipping now and the end result wouldn't be aught that either of them would be able to walk away from unscathed.

CHAPTER TWENTY

THE FOLLOWING MORN Alana did her best to avoid Rory as much as possible. They were continuing their journey and whilst she would love to drag her feet and delay her arrival for longer, she kenned that it was not something that could happen.

She was surprised when Rory entered the cave that morn and declared the trail passable. She had fully intended to have to make camp in the cave for a few days. She was both sad and happy to hear the news. Sad because it meant she was getting closer to her betrothed and happy that she wouldn't have to be stuck inside the small space with Rory, who made it clear that he did not want to be near her. She ignored the pain that revelation caused in her chest.

Her ankle was still quite sore, but her limp was nearly gone. Her movement was slow, but she pushed forward.

Rory walked ahead of her, stony silence emanating from him.

In her mind, she replayed his words from the night afore. The way he snapped when she warned him not to go outside. She had done that out of caring. She didn't want him to become ill, but she supposed he saw it as her mothering him and what grown man wants to be mothered?

She grunted as she climbed over a fallen log, its decaying bark dark from the rain. Ants busily slipped under the bark and then out again.

Staring at Rory's back she couldn't help but wonder why he was pulling away. Suddenly so, it seemed. They had made such progress in their relationship and now, it was as if the rug she'd been standing on had been pulled from beneath her feet, sending her spiraling to the floor.

They came upon a slippery ledge and Rory paused, waiting for her to catch up, then held out his hand so he could help her over it.

Slipping her hand in his, she tried to ignore the familiar heat that radiated up her arm. Just like it did every other time they touched. But as soon as she was over the ledge, he pulled his hand away, and walked ahead, never meeting her eyes. Not saying a word.

The rejection stung and she wasn't sure how to handle it.

"The ground doesnae seem as dampened from the rain up here," she said, trying to initiate a conversation. It was a bad attempt, though, because he only grunted and continued walking.

"How much longer do ye think we have until we arrive?" She asked, thinking he couldn't really dodge that question.

"Two days, mayhap three," he answered, his voice clipped as he lengthened his stride to take him further ahead of her.

She sighed. Mayhap it was the weather that had him in such a dour mood. Or mayhap he was tired, she told herself. She was well aware that he had not been sleeping well the past few nights. For various reasons not entirely kenned to her.

Coming to the conclusion that he wasn't going to engage in any small talk with her, she gave up on trying. Why bother if he was only going to ignore her?

But as they walked on, her heart grew heavy and then heavier with each step. She realized she missed him walking beside her. Talking to her. His rare smile that he kept hidden. His even rarer laughter. All those things combined to make one amazing man and she missed him. Not just his presence—she missed him. The truth settled in her chest like a lead weight. Bringing her down, down, down. If she were in the loch, she would drown from the force of it dragging her to the sandy bottom.

She only wanted to hear him laugh again. His deep laugh that sent shivers down her spine in the most delicious of ways. She wanted to feel the rumble of his chest against her skin. She wanted to hear the steady thump, thump, thump of his heart under her cheek.

Her limbs felt heavy and for a moment she felt like she might faint. She paused, watching his form fade into the distance. But she didn't call out to him. If he didn't want her near him, she for certs would not force herself upon him. She sat on a large rock nearby and swiped at the tear that rolled down her cheek.

She was acting daft. Why was she crying? For Rory? For a man she could never have because she was promised to another. Sometimes she really disliked the life she lived. The feeling of being a pawn was not something that made someone feel wanted. Quite the opposite, actually, she thought.

A few long moments passed afore Rory appeared in her vision, his brows drawn down in worry.

"Are ye unweel?" He asked, dropping in front of her, concern lacing his voice.

She shook her head.

"Then why have ye stopped?"

"I found myself growing tired and needed a respite."

He pushed his hands through his hair and then pulled at his neck. "Ye should have called out for me. If I hadnae looked back and noticed, ye would have been abandoned."

She smiled, but she felt no humor. "'Twould no' be the first time. Mayhap now ye ken why I was abandoned in the first place."

Rory scoffed. "Dinnae say such things."

"And pray tell, why no'? 'Tis no' as if ye care." Her words sounded biting even to her own ears. "Ye were walking far ahead of me. I could have fallen to my death and ye wouldnae have noticed."

He gave her a droll look. "Ye are being ridiculous."

"Am I?" She asked incredulously. "I think no'. I ken ye have grown tired of me. Of escorting me. 'Twould be much easier to leave me behind."

He dropped onto the rock beside her, his shoulder and arm resting against hers. She tried to ignore how much she missed the closeness. How much she enjoyed his presence every time he was near.

"I dinnae blame ye for it. I understand and would react in much the same way if our roles were reversed," she confessed.

His gaze slammed into hers. "Why do ye say such things? If I had wanted to leave ye behind, I would have done so long ago." He rubbed the back of his neck.

"Why didnae ye?"

Green eyes bore into hers, searching her face for what only he kenned. The walls that usually surrounded him were up again and Alana feared she would not be penetrating them anytime soon. Mayhap never.

He laughed, annoyance lifting the corners of his full lips, and he shook his head. "Ye dinnae see aught with those pretty eyes of yers."

His words took her aback. "Ye think my eyes are pretty?" No one had ever told her that.

With a roll of his eyes, he nodded. "How could I no'? I would have to be blind no' to see."

She smiled at his compliment. At the happiness it made her feel. She leaned into him. "What are we?" She asked.

It took Rory a long time to answer. So long that Alana did not think he would. Finally, he said, "Two lost souls."

She thought about that. Were they lost? Was she lost? She hadn't thought so when she was home at Auchenford. She was happy with the life she led there. It was sheltered, aye, much more so than she wanted, but her father always said it was for her protection—to ensure her safety. She accepted his answer. She had no reason not to, really.

She had not realized what life was like outside of the walls of

Auchenford. That life existed outside of the shelter she had grown accustomed to.

But she had been thinking about her time at her former home a lot lately. The life she lived then, she can see now, wasn't as what had been explained to her. Nay, she was a prisoner in her home. She could go nowhere alone. Her maid was always with her. Guards watched over her every minute of the day. Searching her memory, she could not think of one instance when she wasn't surrounded by them. Thinking about it now, it made no sense.

When her parent's hosted visitors from other clans or even the English every so often, Alana was never allowed to come down from her room. Her door was actually locked to prevent her from doing so. But, again, her father stated it was for her safety and well-being. Always for her safety.

However, looking back, she wondered if it was because he didn't want her mingling with the guests. The young men that would accompany their fathers. There were many, but not once had Alana ever said a word to one of them. She could only watch from her chamber window as they arrived or left.

Was her father purposely hiding her away so she wouldn't become enamored with one of the visitors, or so that one of the visitors didn't ask for her hand?

She nibbled at her fingernail. That didn't make sense. Some of those visiting would have made great matches. Their clans combined would create a mighty force and it would keep her close to home.

"What has yer mind so occupied, Bluebell?" Rory asked softly beside her, nudging her shoulder gently.

Not wanting to burden him with her problems, she shook her head. "'Tis naught." She pushed off the rock, immediately missing his warmth. "We should probably continue on. I am for certs there is much ground we need to cover afore stopping for the night and my ankle has slowed us enough in our travels."

A look that she couldn't decipher crossed Rory's face, but he quickly masked his expression. "Ye are right." With a sigh he stood, picked up their packs, and led the way for them to carry on.

He had slowed the pace of his strides compared to earlier in the day when they had been walking. She was having an easier time keeping up with him, even with her sore ankle, which was still tightly wound in the strips of cloth Rory had applied.

They both walked quietly once again, each of them lost in their own thoughts. She was unsure of what plagued his mind, but hers was haunted by all things Rory.

Alana wanted him to laugh so she could hear his deep rumble again. Her mind kept wandering to when he'd carried her with such ease and care when she'd twisted her ankle. He'd picked her up afore she could put up a fight, acting as if she had weighed naught. As if she were no match for his strength. But most of all, he acted as if she mattered. In that moment she felt as if she was Rory's world.

And she enjoyed that very much.

And now, she missed that very much.

Later, after Rory had once again made camp and cooked them a meal that consisted of partridge that he had hunted with his bow, the silence stretched long and quiet betwixt them. Neither of them wanting to say what was on their minds.

Their journey was coming to an end. She could feel it in the way he was pulling away from her.

And she hated it.

Rory joined her by the fire, dropping beside her. She didn't say a word. The flames were her focus, and her eyes didn't stray from the crackling fire. The one time she dared sneak a peek at him, his lips were pressed into a thin line, his forearms resting on his knees as he, too, stared into the flames.

She didn't speak.

Neither did he.

And Alana came to the conclusion that the silence betwixt them was worse than any storm they would weather.

It was a torture she didn't want to take part in.

Did he feel the same? She would never ken, because it wasn't a question she would ever ask him.

$$\longleftarrow \!\!\!\! \bullet \!\!\!\! - \!\!\!\! - \!\!\!\! \bullet \!\!\!\! \longrightarrow$$

CHAPTER TWENTY-ONE

HE CLOUDS HAD cleared enough that Rory could see the stars as he rested his head on his open palms and stared up at the sky. Alana slept peacefully beside him. Close enough to touch, but he restrained himself from doing so, just as he had many times since he'd first met her.

It mattered naught how much he wanted to.

She stirred and his gaze slid to her. She slept on her side, which seemed to be her favorite position, her hands tucked under her cheek. A lock of her hair fell across her eyes.

He sighed, wishing things were different. Different circumstances. A different time. A different place.

Just different.

"Can ye no' sleep?" she whispered, pushing the hair out of her face, and pushing up to rest on her arm. "Ye should try," she urged when he shook his head no.

Just beyond the perimeter of the light of the fire, there was a rustle in the brush. A distinct rustle that Rory kenned well. He stiffened and Alana sat up, immediately realizing something was amiss.

"What is it?" she asked, her voice low as her eyes, wide with fear, scanned the darkness.

He moved to her side, and instinctively, he moved her behind him as he grabbed his dagger, standing at the ready just as a wild boar charged them from the undergrowth. Behind him, Alana screamed as the beast rumbled toward them, snorting angrily as it gnashed its teeth.

Pushing Alana out of harm's way, he yelled to her. "Stay down," he shouted as he struck out at the beast, his blade sinking into its shoulder as the animal roared, kicking out and swinging its large head to and fro. Rory jumped back out of the way of its sharp tusks, trying not to get stabbed.

When it charged again, he swung his blade once more, this time hitting the boar in its rear flank. With a yelp, he thundered through their camp, nearly running into the fire, afore he disappeared into the woods on the other side, the sound of breaking branches echoing in its wake.

Rory ran to Alana, dropping to the ground beside her. His heart racing in his chest as he looked her over, checking her for wounds. Both of their breaths coming in short gasps.

"W-w-will he come back?" Her voice wavered, she was scared to death. It was evident in her pale face and her round eyes.

"Nay, we are safe. Are ye hurt?" He asked, worry making his question come out in a rough voice. As he waited for her to answer, he checked her for injuries, his hands roaming over her arms, her waist, her legs, taking care for her already injured ankle.

She shook her head.

He breathed a sigh of relief. She was fine, but she trembled violently.

Grasping his shirt in her fists, she whispered, "Ye could have been killed." The pain and worry in her voice were like a punch to the gut. It was the realization that she was just as scared that he had been harmed as he was for her.

It was an awakening that seemed to take over his soul.

She cared for him. The way she was clinging to his shirt, looking up at him with her beautiful hazel eyes boring into his. It was then he kenned. The dawning of what was growing betwixt them that had him wanting more. Without thinking of the consequences or not caring about what the consequences would be, his mouth was on hers afore he could stop himself. His need raw and desperate.

Alana kissed him back, wrapping her arms around his neck, and he reveled in the feeling of her. The taste of her. His tongue explored her mouth as if he was discovering a new land, and she let him. Sighing into him as her body relaxed flush against his, as her fists clutched at him.

He lowered them to the blankets, not breaking the kiss. He wasn't ready for that yet. He didn't care that he was desperate for air. He was desperate for Alana's touch even more. Her kiss. Her mouth. Her taste.

She was lying on her back, he on his side next to her when they finally broke apart. Each of them gasping, their chests heaving. He was breathing so hard, he didn't think he would ever recover. He rested his forehead against hers, fighting a war within himself that crossed the line of what he wanted to do and what he kenned was right.

"This shouldnae have happened," he said, hating the words as they left his lips. They tasted sour, bitter. Like the lies they were.

Alana didn't say aught. She didn't tell him to back away. To stop touching her. To leave her alone. Instead, she reached up and, with a gentle hand, stroked his cheek. Rory closed his eyes and leaned into her soft touch.

It was heaven.

Neither of them moved. They stayed that way until Rory thought he was going to scream in desperation. In want.

When Alana lifted and pressed her lips against his, Rory kenned there was no going back. He would not return from this. He wasn't sure he wanted to. He only kenned that he wanted to lose himself in Alana Duran more than aught he had ever wanted in his life afore.

He scooped her up in his arms, and she wrapped her legs around him with a squeal. "Where are we going?" She asked, her voice husky.

Kissing the tip of her nose, he smiled. "Ye'll see."

He carried her through the trees, to a spring that he kenned was near there. It drained into a crystal blue pool of water.

"'Tis beautiful," she said, craning her neck to peer into the water. The spring wasn't large, nor was the pool. Instead, they offered an intimate place for two people to splash around, amongst other things. But most importantly, the small size of the pool meant that the water wouldn't be nearly as cold as other, larger bodies.

Setting Alana down on her feet, careful not to agitate her ankle, he smiled and tugged off his tunic. "Ye can say nay. I willnae be angry."

With wide eyes, she shook her head, tentatively reaching out her hands, her tongue darting out to wet her lips. Her fingertips brushed over his pectorals, making the muscles jump. She flattened her hands so her palms were splayed out over his skin as she dragged them down, lower, to his abdominal muscles, which contracted under her touch. He bit back the groan her touch elicited. He snatched her hands up and kissed her fingers greedily.

"Yer fingers are like magic, bewitching me until I cannae think straight."

She gave him a wicked smile. "I believe I rather like the sound of that."

"Ye are a naughty minx, Bluebell." He pulled her closer and was happy that she allowed it and didn't push away. Instead, she wrapped her arms around his neck, pulling him down to her so their lips could touch, gently, softly. So different from the feelings warring inside of him. He didn't want gentle. He didn't want soft. He wanted to capture her mouth in a deep kiss that would leave nay doubt of his feelings for her. He wanted to drive into her heat and lose himself in the sensation of her milking his cock.

Alana stepped away, dipping her head, and looking up at him through lowered lashes. She lifted her skirts, slowly revealing her legs as she raised them higher and higher. The pale, smooth skin of her calves teased him first, afore her knees were bared, and then, Rory sucked in a breath betwixt his teeth, her thighs. His breath escaped in a sharp hiss.

Noticing his reaction, Alana's smile grew wider, then she dropped her skirts and covered all the treasure she had just so brazenly uncovered for him to get a glimpse at.

"Ye tease me," he accused.

"Do I? I think no'."

He reached out and pulled her to him. "Ye do. I dinnae like it," he growled, and nuzzled her neck.

She pushed off his chest. "Ye didnae like what ye saw?" Her brows furrowed and she looked hurt.

"Och, no' like ye are thinking. I enjoyed what I saw verra much. I didnae like it when ye hid yerself from my gaze."

"Ah," she purred, and the sound went straight to his hardening manhood, straining against his trews. "'Tis a reason for that."

"Aye?" He questioned.

Alana nodded. "Surely, ye dinnae think I can pull my skirts o'er my head." She chuckled. "Nay, I must slide them down my hips."

Rory closed his eyes on a groan at her words. Did she ken how much her talk was making his body roar to life?

"Do ye need help with such a task?" He asked, his voice a hoarse whisper.

She tilted her head, meeting his gaze, and then looked toward the water, and shivered. "It looks cold."

"'Tis no'. The water here is actually quite warm. I believe ye will find it refreshing."

She lifted a brow as if she didn't believe him.

"'Tis true. The springs used to be a hot spring, howe'er o'er the years, they've lessened. Now they're warm, but quite pleasant."

He waited, letting her decide on what she wanted to do. He would force her into naught, so each move would be her own. Each decision her own. He was giving her the gift of choice. Something no one in her life had given her afore. But that didn't mean he wasn't saying a silent prayer that she would agree and soon they would be skin on skin in the warm water.

"Weel, then. I guess we are wasting time, shivering in the cool e'ening air when we could be relaxing in warm waters."

Rory beamed. He couldn't help it.

"Let me assist ye so ye dinnae hurt yer ankle any further."

Alana paused for a moment, and Rory feared that she had changed her mind. But she nodded and lifted her foot, balancing on her good leg, so he could untie her boot. Then she leaned against him so he could do the same for her other leg.

Standing in her bare feet, Rory watched as she slowly untied her belt. Then painfully slowly, she removed her outer garments until she stood in front of him in only her thin shift.

His eyes roamed over her body. He could see the silhouette of her body through the sheer material. It was perfect in every way. From the width of her hips, to the indent of her waist that he could wrap his hands around, to the swell of her breasts.

Perfection.

"Bluebell," he whispered. "Ye are beautiful."

Her cheeks tinged pink, and she caught her lip betwixt her teeth, as she looked at him shyly.

"Yer turn," she said softly.

"With pleasure." He didn't think he had ever undressed so quickly. He'd already removed his tunic, so it was only a matter of removing his boots and trews. As he pushed his trews, down his hips, his hard cock sprung free, bobbing in the air, and he smiled at how Alana's eyes widened.

When he stood in front of her, naked as the day he was born, he took pride in the way Alana's eyes roved over him, pausing on his manhood.

She grasped the hem of her shift and pulled it over her head, revealing her beauty to him and Rory had to wonder how he had gotten so lucky. Briefly, he reminded himself that she couldn't be his, but he pushed the thought out of his head before it could take root and fester.

Instead, he bent and scooped her up in his arms and carried her into the water. She tightened her arms around his neck, and he thought it was because she was worried the water was going to be cold, but he wasn't lying when he told her the water would be warm.

It was and she relaxed in his arms. He let her go, so she could tread water.

"This feels divine, Rory."

"I told ye," he said with a smile afore dunking his head under the water, wetting his hair. He rubbed his hands briskly over his head afore resurfacing.

Alana leaned back, letting her hair soak up the water, and sighed as she looked up at the darkening sky. "How did ye find such an amazing place?"

He shrugged, the water running in rivulets over his shoulders. "I hike through these lands often. I happened upon it years ago and like to think of it is as my own private oasis. 'Tis lovely, is it no'?"

"Aye," she sighed. "I would also keep this to myself. Thank ye for sharing it with me." She swam close to him as he watched, and to his surprise, she sliced her hands through water and splashed him.

"Och!" He laughed as he wiped the water from his face. "Ye didnae just splash me," he said sternly, but there was no ire behind his words.

"Och, aye, I did." And she repeated the motion afore quickly swimming away from him.

If there was one thing Rory enjoyed, it was a chase, and he was more than happy to chase her through the water. She proved to be an adept swimmer, and when he caught her by the waist and spun her around to face him, she squealed afore he silenced her with a deep kiss. She wrapped her legs around his waist, and he groaned as the apex of her thighs rubbed against his hardness.

His tongue explored her mouth, it was his new favorite territory to conquer. Breaking the kiss, he brought his lips to the column of her throat, suckling, nipping, then licking away the sting. He couldn't get enough of her and when he dropped his mouth to her breasts and sucked a taut nipple into his mouth, they groaned at the same time. Alana's fingernails dug into his shoulders, and she threw her head back, her eyes closed in pleasure. The movement thrust her breasts up and forward and Rory lapped at them. Starving. He palmed the globes, massaging them, flicking his thumb across her stiff peaks, the movement had her grinding her hips into him.

"Christ, Bluebell. Do ye have any idea what ye do to me?"

He dropped his hands to her hips, then moved them to her bottom, squeezing, as he ground his pelvis against her, loving the friction, but wanting more. Kenning he shouldn't, but not caring.

Alana was his. Consequences be damned.

Bringing his hand to her front, he found her nestle of curls and the warmth hidden there. He slid a finger through her folds, and sunk in to his knuckle.

She gasped and she clung to his shoulders, her hazel eyes wide. He added another finger, slowly drawing in and out, working her to a frenzy in his arms. He withdrew and added pressure, making slow circles on the small bud of nerves, and she nearly flew out of his arms.

"Rory!" She cried, the sound echoing around them.

Hell, this woman was going to be the death of him.

"I want ye, Bluebell. More than aught I have e'er wanted in my life," he confessed on ragged breaths.

"Take me, Rory. I cannae wait any longer."

He brought his hands up to her face, rubbing his thumbs over her jawline as he met her gaze. "Are ye for certs?"

She nodded, kissing his lips.

"We cannae go back."

"I dinnae want to."

"Yer future, 'twill be ruined." He needed her to ken what the ramifications of her decision would be. He did not want to sway her in any way whatsoever. It was her decision, and hers alone.

Whatever it was, he would respect it. But, damn, he wanted her to say yes.

"I belong to ye, Rory Hart. Ye hold my heart, body, and soul." She slammed her mouth on his, her tongue finding his in the most wicked of dances.

Working his fingers into her, he brought her to the edge of losing herself, and when he felt she was at the precipice of falling to pieces, he entered her. She was so tight, squeezing him as he pushed forward, breaking her barrier. He captured her cry with a kiss and stilled, allowing her to adjust to him. To his size, to the fullness she was feeling.

Tears leaked from the corners of her eyes, and he kissed them away. "I'm so verra sorry, Bluebell. The pain will lessen."

The wait for her to adjust to him was excruciating. He wanted to thrust into her so badly, but he waited. Once again, giving her the lead.

Finally, she began to move slightly, testing how she felt. Her arms were wrapped around his shoulders and, using him as leverage as the warm water surrounded them, she rotated her hips, and his eyes nearly rolled back in his head at the pleasure she elicited.

"I'm ready," she whispered, her voice husky.

He smiled as his mouth met hers and he drew her tighter to him, thrusting his hips. Over and over, the water moved in waves around them, sloshing against them as he lost himself in her warmth. In the sounds of her moans echoing in the glen. His whole body was taut, his muscles bunching, his fingers digging into the skin of Alana's thighs. Her pants grew quicker, and he pushed a hand betwixt their bodies, finding the button of pleasure nerves and circled it, applying pressure, and that did it.

Her body tightened around him, squeezing him almost painfully, heightening his pleasure. Her limbs grew stiff and she threw her head back and yelled his name to the trees. He quickened his pace, driving himself to the ledge so he could jump off and join her.

His bollocks drew up, tightened, and with a final thrust, burying himself to the hilt, he shuddered and ground out his release, spilling his seed into her, clinging to her as they desperately held onto each other.

Alana trembled in his arms. Fierce spasms shaking her body.

"Are ye weel, Bluebell?" He asked, concern lacing his voice, which was shaky from his ragged breathing.

She smiled shyly. "I have ne'er been better."

"We should probably get out of the water. 'Tis warm, but we have been in for quite some time. I doonae want ye to catch a chill."

He carried Alana out of the water and as soon as the cool air hit them, they both shivered. Scooping up their items, they ran with their clothes wrapped around them to the fire that thankfully, still burned bright.

"Take heed of yer ankle, Bluebell," Rory called out.

But she only giggled as they sank onto their blankets and wrapped themselves in them, holding them tightly around them as they sat side by side, warming themselves.

After some time had passed, Rory stretched out on the blanket and brought Alana to nestle by his side, tucking the other blanket around them. "Sleep, Bluebell. We will have much to discuss in the morn."

She remained silent but snuggled closer into him.

He didn't look forward to the morn. They had just made a massive mistake. They let their emotions and bodies rule them and gave in to temptation.

There would be a price to pay.

But worse than that, Rory didn't ken how he would be able to let Alana go now that he had a taste of her.

CHAPTER TWENTY-TWO

A LANA WOKE UP to the sensation of Rory's arm draped over her, weighing her down in a way that made her feel cherished as she never had afore. She shifted under him and her body screamed in protest. She was sore—everywhere. As she lay there, watching the clouds float lazily in the sky above, her thoughts wandered to what they had done. Guilt flooded her. But not regret. Nay, she refused to regret one second of the moments they had shared last eve.

Their coming together was beautiful.

So why was her stomach tumbling at the memory? A feeling of unease settled over her and she fought to tamp it down.

Beside her, Rory stirred. He covered his eyes with his forearm for a moment then he dropped it to his side and his green-eyed gaze met hers. His brows furrowed. He probably sensed the shift in the air around them this morn.

"Good morn," he said, his voice deep and gravelly from sleep. He pushed himself into a sitting position and deftly maneuvered pulling on his trews afore he stood and let the blanket fall, giving her a brief glance of his muscled bottom.

His absence was immediately felt. The air around Alana suddenly cooled without having him nearby.

"Did ye sleep weel?" She asked, curious if he had slept as well as she had. It was one of the best nights of sleep she had ever experienced. Being wrapped safe and warm in Rory's arms all night had felt so right. Everything else, everyone else, fell away and it was just them. The two of them, alone in the world, without a care for aught else.

But now? She wasn't as for certs as she was when she had fallen asleep.

"I did." His answer was clipped, and Alana felt the shift in the air betwixt them. "Ye should dress, we should be on our way soon."

She searched his face, but he was no longer meeting her eyes. Every time she tried to catch his gaze, he looked away.

She nodded, believing that there was naught to say at the moment and dressed as Rory packed their bags for the journey ahead.

A journey that she was now very much regretting. It had always been their plan, but now, with everything that had happened, Alana was dreading her arrival and meeting her future husband.

Later, as they walked, Rory didn't stray far from her side. He stayed near, but also took care not to touch her. He still avoided her eyes. His closeness had the hairs on her arms raised, her skin like gooseflesh. Her heart skipping a beat each time she caught him stealing a glance her way. She couldn't stop thinking about him. His scent assaulted her senses. It was like he was wrapped in the outdoors, a heady mix of pine, fresh air, and heather. She took a deep breath, inhaling deeply, committing it to memory so she would never forget.

She missed the warmth he offered when he held her like he never wanted to let her go. Did he feel the same way? She stole her own sideways glance at him. His eyes flicked away quickly, and she sighed as her heart once again skipped a beat. Focusing on the trail ahead, Rory consumed all of her thoughts. It didn't matter that she tried to ignore him beside her. To ignore their time spent together last eve. He was the only thing on her mind. Her fingers still remembered touching him. The heat that emanated from him. The way he would hiss as she trailed her fingers down his abdomen, leaving a trail of gooseflesh in their wake. Her own body remembered his touch. Yearned to feel it again. His searing fingers and the way they made her feel as if she were aflame. Just the thought of what they had done had her body longing for him again. She wanted him to capture her mouth in his. To claim her as his again.

She let out a slow breath and chewed her lower lip. Sadness causing tears to prick at her eyes. Would they ever be together?

Of course not. The wave of guilt she felt earlier returned. Hanging over her like a massive weight dragging her down. What would her betrothed think when he found out? For certs he would not want to go through with the marriage.

A little of the weight lifted. If he refused to marry her, then she would be free to be with Rory. Nay, she must marry. Stepping over a fallen log, she lost her balance and Rory quickly reached out to steady her. This time when his eyes met with hers, he didn't draw them away. Instead, it was as if they bore into her, trying to read her thoughts.

How she wished she could tell him all that was circling in her head.

"Are ye weel?" He asked, concern etched across his face.

Alana almost didn't want to answer, kenning as soon as she did, he would let go and break the connection. But she couldn't not say aught without appearing daft, so she nodded. "Thank ye."

As expected, he let go of her arm, her hand falling limply to her side, and she wanted to scream. *Touch me! Hold me!* But she couldn't.

Images of her upcoming wedding flooded her mind. She supposed her chests of items and her wardrobe had already been delivered to her betrothed's estate. Everything would be there waiting for her, and she didn't want to go. For the first time in her life, she cared naught for the items she had packed to accompany her to her new home. What good were items, really? They offered naught. She had managed just fine with the few clothes she brought with her that Rory carried in her sack. Why did she need expensive gowns when all she would do was sit inside and be miserable?

There was only one answer to that question.

She didn't.

But she had to go. The choice wasn't hers. Her father had agreed to the union. Her clan depended on her going through with the marriage. It guaranteed their safety.

But for how long? For the first time, she questioned her father's antics and whether or not he was doing the best of jobs when it came to leading their clan to a fruitful existence. From what she could piece together, he wasn't. She thought back to her childhood. Whilst she and her brothers had been given all they had needed, their clansfolk were oft left wanting. Whether it be for food or shelter, they were always in need.

Then her father would strike a deal with another clan and things would improve for a while. When they no longer were, another deal would be struck and things would move on in the right direction again, until it wasn't. Over and over the cycle repeated itself. How had she not recognized the pattern afore?

And now she was all that was left. Her father's last bargaining chip.

She clenched her fists at her sides. The man was not a good leader. If he was, they wouldn't find themselves in this position over and over again. How long would the coin he received from her marriage last? If his past deals were taken into consideration, not long at all. Then what? He had naught left to bargain with.

And what would happen to her clan? They would fall into ruin. Families would starve or freeze to death unless they decided to be absorbed into another clan.

So everything that awaited her with Michael MacDonell? It was all temporary. Not her marriage. Nay, that was eternal. But her clan's safety? That would not be long-lived.

"Bluebell?" Rory paused and turned to her. "Ye seem," he paused, shifting from one foot to the other. "Angry."

She squared her shoulders, jutting her chin out defiantly as she met his gaze. "I am." She admitted, stomping her foot on the ground, not caring that she looked like a petulant child. "I am angry. Furious, to be honest."

"What can I do?"

His question took her by surprise. He hadn't asked what he had done, which was naught, of course. But, instead, he was asking how he could be of help. She threw her hands up in defeat and shook her head. Could this man that she couldn't have be any more perfect?

"'Tis naught that ye can do. Just like there is naught I can do." She kicked at a loose rock on the trail. "It, it angers me so," she finally said and stomped off, her fists clenched at her sides.

Within seconds Rory caught up with her, causing her to pause when he held her shoulders and forced her to look at him. And that was when she saw it.

The pain he had been hiding. It was written all over his face as he looked at her. "Is it because of last eve?" He asked quietly, his voice shaking.

She couldn't believe big, strong, Rory Hart wasn't fearless. Alana didn't think there was aught that could make him afraid. But as he stood there, watching her, his eyes searching hers, she kenned he was feeling the weight of what they'd done. And how they could fix it.

She shook her head and pushed him away, but he held her tight, not letting her go.

"Tell me," he ordered, his voice low. His fingertips squeezed into her upper arms.

She huffed out a breath. "Nay. That is no' what angers me." She threw her hands up in the air and let them fall to her sides with a smack. "How could I regret the best night of my life?"

The tension in his shoulders relaxed a bit, but he still looked concerned. "I am happy to hear that but saddened that something else bothers ye. Talk to me, Bluebell. Ye can tell me aught."

"I dinnae want to marry MacDonell. I dinnae want to be used

as barter for something that my father will just waste away and it will all be for naught. Just like e'ery other deal he has struck in the past. In a year, mayhap two, when my clan is in the same position they are now, then all my sacrifices will have been for naught. I see that now. And it infuriates me." She swiped angrily at a tear that began to roll down her cheek.

"Och, Bluebell. Come here." He pulled her to him and wrapped his strong arms around her. "I am sorry." He kissed the top of her head as he held her and how she wished he would kiss her lips instead.

Imagining her wedding, she felt naught of the desire she felt for the man holding her now. There was no spark when she thought of MacDonell. No flame or burning passion. Just a cold, gray void of the misery that awaited her once they spoke their vows. It all felt hollow. So hollow and she didn't ken how to handle that.

She had never met the man and, yet, she could easily see their future together. A horrible future in a loveless marriage. What kind of man would pay her father for her hand? It was the opposite of how marriage contracts worked. She should have had a dowry, a large one at that, considering her father's station. But she didn't. She wasn't sure she ever had one. So MacDonell was in essence, purchasing her. Like cattle.

Was he such a vile man that the only way he could attain a wife was to buy her?

She pressed her cheek to Rory's chest, and inhaled his scent as she squeezed him tight, wishing she never had to let him go.

Later that night, as they sat on opposite sides of the fire, not trusting themselves to sit near each other again, she found the bundle of parchment she had hastily packed, and penned a missive to her betrothed.

Rory watched her, that same pain in her heart, shining through in his eyes, as she wrote. He didn't ken what she wrote, and he didn't ask out of respect for her. But she needed to cleanse herself of the thoughts running through her mind. Thoughts of her marriage. Of the MacDonell whom she had never even met. Of Rory. How she didn't want to leave his side. She didn't ken how she would survive without him. About how the only thing she saw in her future was a bleak loneliness.

She didn't sign it. She couldn't. She doubted that the letter would ever make it out of her possession. It was best that it didn't. The consequences would be dire for both she and Rory if it did. And she wouldn't do that to him. As much as she wanted to spend the rest of her days with him, she kenned she couldn't. She had been promised to another and had to fulfill her commitment, no matter how much it pained her. How miserable her future would be. It mattered naught.

When Rory presented her to Michael MacDonell, she would follow through with her duty, and she would set Rory free. Because he deserved to be happy.

Unable to sleep, she lay awake, looking at the stars and whispered, "What am I doing?"

The universe didn't answer though.

Her heart did. And the only answer that felt right was—falling.

                              ━━◄•━━━━━━━━•►━━

CHAPTER TWENTY-THREE

RORY WOKE EARLY the next morn, his heart heavy. He hadn't slept well. Not with thoughts of Alana constantly in his head. He kenned what the feeling was that had him in such a chokehold. He couldn't deny it. As much as he should. As much as he needed to.

He couldn't.

Sitting on a rock, he watched as Alana braided her long, thick hair. She was humming softly to herself. The tune sad, heartfelt. He wondered if she kenned the complete mess she had made of him. He didn't think so. She was completely unaware of just how much of an effect she had on him.

When they walked, unhurriedly, since Rory kenned they were getting close and he wanted to delay their arrival as much as possible, he found deer tracks in the mud.

"Look at these," he called out, pausing and pointing so Alana could see them.

"What are they?" She asked curiously.

"Deer tracks." He followed them for a bit, to the edge of the trees, where berry bushes grew. "They stopped here to eat the berries." He dipped his head toward the woods. "Then entered the trees. If ye follow them, they will lead ye to water."

"How do ye ken?" She asked, interested.

"They always do. They'll eat, drink, and then burrow down

someplace safe, away from predators." He looked around. "Here." He pointed out more tracks in the mud left behind from the earlier storms. She approached, studying them.

"What are those from?"

"Hare. See, ye can see how they zig zag? 'Tis their defense against predators. 'Tis more difficult for them to be caught when they hop from side to side instead of in a straight line." He stood up. "We can follow them, and ye'll see." He turned her shoulders and pointed her toward the woods. "Can ye see where they go?"

She studied the ground, her head tilted to the side, and moved in the wrong direction.

Rory chuckled, and corrected her direction. "This way," he pointed to the ground, showing her each indent the hare had made in the mud.

She shifted and his arm brushed against hers, their fingers touching.

Heat flared betwixt them, but he stepped back quickly.

"Er, ye'll need these tracking skills when ye go back," he said, pulling on the back of his neck. "In case ye e'er return."

Her face fell. "Return? What do ye mean?"

He refused to meet her eyes. Not when he kenned he would see longing that matched his own there.

Once again, he reminded himself that she isn't his to want. It was the same thing he had been repeating to himself over and over again. Mayhap if he said it enough, he would start to believe it.

He didn't ken who he was fooling. Definitely not himself. He kenned it didn't matter how many times he repeated the mantra. He still wouldn't believe it.

Growing serious, he took a deep breath and spoke from his heart. "When I was ordered to escort ye to yer betrothed, I had no choice but to agree. Duty above all else, as we have both apparently, been told. I tried to keep my distance." He laughed, but it wasn't comical. "It was hard. So damn hard. Ye caught me as soon as ye spoke with sass and confidence. From that moment, ye had me enthralled. Enchanted."

Her eyes rounded as she listened to his heartfelt confession.

"There may have been times where ye believe I was annoyed. I pray ye realize I wasnae. I was waging a war within myself. One that is still being waged with e'ery breath I take. E'ery time I glance upon ye." He pushed his hands through his hair roughly.

"I will get ye to yer betrothed," he said quietly. "Just as promised. E'en though doing so will absolutely tear me in two. The thought of delivering ye to another man that will take ye as wife rips me open with a pain as such I have ne'er experienced afore. Right here." He rubbed the left side of his chest, just over his heart.

Alana stepped forward, laying her palms flat on his chest as she looked up it him, the pain that he was for certs in his own eyes, reflected in hers.

He wanted to curse the world. How could it be so cruel? How could he have found the one woman that he could see a future with—as his wife, as the mother of his bairns—only for her to be unavailable to him?

"Rory," she said softly, her fingers clutching at his tunic. "We could run."

He shook his head. "Dinnae say such things." It was desperation that made her say such a statement. It was the realization of how close they were to her new home. The dread that the time spent in each other's company was nearing an end.

"Ye ken the Highlands like the back of yer hand. We could make our home here. Far away from anyone else. They would ne'er be able to find us. Please!" She said hopefully, as he took hold of her hands in his and brought them up to his lips so he could kiss each fingertip softly.

"As much as I love that idea, we both ken we cannae. We will have no' only our families looking for us, but the MacDonell as weel. They would find us."

She pulled her hands away and swiped at the fat tears that fell over her cheeks like a fast flowing waterfall, shaking her head in denial.

Watching her break down in front of him felt like a stab to his heart. A searing pain that split open his chest and exposed him to the world. A burning fire that was opposite of the inferno her body ignited in him. He wanted to give in. To run away with her as she suggested. But deep down, they both kenned they could not.

Duty, which they each had, needed to be fulfilled. It mattered naught what their hearts wanted.

"Bluebell," he pleaded, hating the sound of desperation in his own voice. "We need to do what we must."

Continuing to shake her head vehemently, she broke out into a full sob. "Nay. Nay. There has to be something we can do. A way to change what has been set in motion."

Rory clenched his jaw. He couldn't lie to her, even though he wanted to by telling her that everything was going to be fine. That in the end, all would settle in their favor. It wouldn't, so he would not tell her it would. He respected her too much to fill her with false hope.

Opening his arms, she fell into them, crying against his chest. He held her like that for a long time as he waited for her tears to subside. Now, her chest heaved uncontrollably against him, but there was no more moisture wetting his tunic. She had cried herself dry.

That night, as they lay under the stars side by side, arms wrapped around each other even though they kenned they shouldn't, Rory watched her sleep.

In the moonlight, he could see her eyes moving rapidly under her closed lids. Every so oft she would kick out a leg, or throw a punch, then whimper.

He took a deep breath. This was torture. He had never spent a night in a dungeon, but he was for certs that it couldn't be worse than what he was experiencing right now. Having his heart ripped out of his chest and having it stomped upon.

Alana shivered, and sniffled as she continued to sleep. He hugged her closer, guarding her body as best he could so she could get through the night. She needed her sleep. On the morrow, they would reach the outskirts of the city, and then his protection would no longer be able to help her.

He would have no choice but to let her go.

His heart forever broken.

Chapter Twenty-Four

T HE SIGHT OF fences and farms in the distance after days of traveling should have brought joy and relief to Alana. But today, it did not. Seeing the smoke curling from chimneys in the distance slowed her steps. The joy she had begun to feel again at having Rory by her side had slipped away once again.

Her smile faded as she realized their final destination was close. Too close. Would Rory stop her if she turned and ran in the opposite direction? She sighed. He would catch her in a matter of strides and though she didn't believe that he would drag her kicking and screaming to deliver her to her betrothed, he would indeed fulfill the duty he had been tasked with.

Just as she must do.

She could smell the burning peat from the cluster of thatched-roof cottages looming closer with every step she took. The sky was filled with gray clouds and drizzle would for certs fall on them afore the day was over. It was *dreich* day and it matched the shift of moods she was experiencing.

"Do ye ken aught aboot the city where my future husband lives?"

"Aye. On the other side of the village ye can see from here, there is a ridge, and then a valley. We'll camp at the ridge this eve, and in the morning cross the valley and into Caercon where the MacDonell castle, Caer Rannoch, stands." His voice was even as he spoke, emotionless.

Whilst she had let her emotions have free range over her reactions since she had broken down the day afore, Rory had been the exact opposite. He had not only masked his emotions, he seemed to have been able to shut them off completely. Alana envied him for that. How she wished she could do the same.

They passed through the streets of the village, even passing an inn, but unlike they had done afore, they did not stop and ask for a room.

Alana understood why. Being in the same room together would end in disaster. They wouldn't be able to stay away from each other or hide the feelings each of them felt for the other. Not only that, the villagers were under the MacDonell's rule. Every move she and Rory did would be watched with the eye of a hawk. Aught that they might do would be reported to her betrothed. Any reaction. Any emotion. All would be told. And that would not bode well for them.

Nay, it would be a much better situation for them to make camp this night where it was just the two of them and the surrounding trees and animals as company.

She would savor this last night alone with Rory. She wanted to memorize every inch of him. The feel of him. The scent of him. All of him.

The people in the village watched them with wary eyes as they walked though. She could understand that. They were outsiders. She remembered how the villagers of Dornich looked at her when her carriage had crashed. It was much the same here, but she felt it was Rory that they were more wary of. He wore the colors of the Hart. From what she had learned from Rory, the clans were not at odds with each other, but the Harts didn't usually travel to them either. So his presence was surprising. If aught, the villagers would have expected to see only Duran colors.

Many whispered behind their hands as she and Rory passed. Alana ignored them, holding her head high. She supposed in due time she would rule over this village alongside her soon-to-be husband. She sighed. The position held no interest for her.

They arrived at the ridge that overlooked the valley just as Rory had promised. Alana stood on the edge looking past the valley at the castle that stood atop an outcropping of rock. It looked dark and fierce. Foreboding. Cold. It was not welcoming in anyway. Was that how she would feel when she arrived? Unwelcome.

Rory, as he did every night when they camped, busied himself with unpacking their gear, starting a fire, and finding food. They had fresh water since they had stopped at a burn not far from here. And Rory had slipped inside one of the pubs they passed and exited with a skin full of ale.

She picked up their folded blankets and shook them out, laying them flat next to each other. This was their last night together. She would not spend it on opposite sides of the fire.

The estate looming in the distance kept demanding her attention.

Sitting with her back against a rock, she fished the letter she had written out of her pocket and read it over again. She wasn't sure what else to add to it. She felt she had already written everything she had to say. The question would be if she would give the letter to Rory or if she would hold on to it and burn it the first chance she got.

Her betrothed could never get his hands on it. That would be disaster for both she and Rory. And in no way did she ever want Rory to be in any sort of danger. Especially because of her. Everything they had shared betwixt them she had played a willing part in. The choice and final decision was hers. She wasn't forced. But she was for certs that the man that was to be her husband would not take such things into consideration.

With a heavy sigh, she shoved the folded paper back into her pocket.

Rory returned with some berries and a small fowl, already dressed, so they only needed to roast it over the fire.

When it was cooked and Rory sat quietly beside her as they ate, melancholy overcame her. He was acting distant again, pulling away from her, and kenning that this was their last night together, the pain of it cut deeper than afore. She didn't want there to be a divide betwixt them.

Popping a wild berry into her mouth, she contemplated how she should word the question she was about to ask him. She slid a gaze over to Rory. He was staring solemnly into the fire, shadows from the flames dancing across his face. His brows were drawn down and his lips were pressed into a thin line. His jawline kept moving and she could see that he was clenching and unclenching it.

Mayhap he was having just as hard a time as she was adjusting and accepting what was going to happen on the morrow.

"Will ye stay with me until I reach the gates?" She finally asked, her voice quiet. She was almost afraid to ask, fashing that he might say nay, that he would not.

To her relief, he nodded. "Of course." But something in his voice was final. Like everything was over now. All that they had shared. It was all in the past never to be revisited again.

Alana shifted her gaze from Rory's face to the fire, her heart breaking into tiny little pieces that scattered like stars in the sky. Far and wide, so they could never be put back together again. Never be whole again. Was she really going to give him up once she arrived at the door of what was supposed to be her new home? Could she really let him go?

Could he let her go?

Nay, she didn't think either of them could.

But what were their choices?

That night, as they covered themselves with their blankets, Alana turned into Rory's chest, placing a kiss on his heart. "I dinnae want this to end," she whispered. "No' now. No' e'er." Just then a gust of wind blew through the trees and over them, pushing her hair into her face.

Strong arms pulled her close and held her tightly and Rory

kissed the top of her head. "Some things are out of our hands, no matter how much we want to change them."

Alana drew circles over his pectorals with her fingertips and dropped her lips to Rory's chest. Kissing him softly, letting the hairs of his chest tickle her nose.

"Bluebell," he murmured, his voice sounding strained.

She lifted her skirts, straddling his thighs and leaned forward, capturing his lips in a kiss that she would emblazon on her memory. "Just give me this one more night, Rory. Give me something that I can remember with fondness when I am stuck in that prison with no escape. Please."

He blew out a shaky breath. "We shouldnae, but dammit, Love, I cannae deny ye for I yearn for the same." He shifted under her, and she felt the hardness of his length as he lined it up with her entrance. Lifting his hips, he entered her on a throaty moan and she gasped at the completely new sensation this offered, compared to the last time they lay together. His hands on her hips, he lifted her and lowered her until she figured out the rhythm and with a newfound confidence, took over the pacing. Lifting up with her thighs, and then slowly sinking back down onto his length. His hardness filled her, and she reveled in the feeling, squeezing around him.

"That's it, Bluebell. Ride me, Love," he sighed.

Love. It was the second time he'd called her that. It warmed her heart at the same time it sliced it open, kenning it wasn't something that she would hear from his lips again after this night.

Rory sat up, bringing their chests together and wrapped his arms around her. His chest hair tickled her breasts, and this new position once again, changed the feeling of their lovemaking. She wanted to learn all she could from him. She wanted him to be the one to teach her all the ways to satisfy him.

Her thighs grew tired, and Rory sensed it. Grasping her hips, he lifted her with ease afore bringing her down on his hardness. He was hard as steel. Their pace quickened. Their moans growing louder. She gasped for air as she felt that familiar pressure build in her stomach, circling, growing, building. That inferno that she desired. She was so close to it exploding from her, she could feel her limbs start to contract, to stiffen, she leaned forward and sank her teeth into his shoulder and a deep growl spilled from his lips as he shifted, pushing her over.

On her back, Rory had full control which he took full advantage of, thrusting into her, over and over, burying himself until he was fully seated in her. He'd stay that way for a long moment afore pulling away and then repeating the process.

His movements drove her mad. She scored his back with her fingernails as she went tumbling over the precipice, falling, falling, all the whilst she screamed his name into the night. Stars exploded in her eyes, brilliant bursts of color like naught she had ever seen afore. Her breath ragged, escaping her mouth in gasps.

With one final hard, deep thrust, Rory crushed her to him, crying out her name, "Bluebell!" As he shuddered violently, spending himself in her, a series of shivers following his release.

He pulled his face back from the crook of her neck so he could see her face. "I ken I shouldnae say it, but I love ye, Bluebell."

Tears pricked her eyes and she nodded. "And I, ye, Rory Hart. I love ye with all my soul." Their mouths crashed together, his tongue running along the seam of her lips until she opened them and he thrust inside her mouth. Their tongues doing a wicked dance to rival their coupling.

"I dinnae ken how I am going to let ye go," he confessed, his voice pained.

She buried her face in his chest. "I dinnae want to think aboot it. I only want to think of us this night. The morrow is a new day. Let us enjoy this night. Let us enjoy each other."

That was what they did. Sleep wasn't had that night. And Alana didn't regret a single second of the time they spent exploring each other's bodies. Painting them to memory to look upon when they were forced to part.

CHAPTER TWENTY-FIVE

RORY AND ALANA walked the final mile in tense silence, the castle looming ahead. He was having a hard time keeping his emotions in check the closer they got. Him losing his composure would only make things harder for Alana and she was already going to have a rough time as it was.

Of the two of them, she would be the one paying the worst price. Whilst he would be forever lonely with only the memory of Alana to keep him warm at night, she was being forced into a marriage she didn't want, to a man she didn't love. And that wasn't even the worst of it. The MacDonell wouldn't treat her like the lady Alana deserved to be treated as. Nay, the man would use her to birth bairns and naught more.

Rory closed his eyes and took a steadying breath. This wasn't his fight. Nor was it the Harts. But, hell, if he didn't want to raze the castle and burn it to the ground with the MacDonell in it. Alana deserved so much more. She deserved to be happy. To live a life of luxury and happiness, with a husband that doted upon her, with children that loved her. She should be treasured.

He clenched his jaw. There were so many things he wanted to say. So many things he wanted to do, but he couldn't. He felt helpless.

They were nearing the gate and it took all of his strength not to pull her to him. To crash his mouth onto hers and claim her for all to see. That way there would be nay doubt who she belonged to.

"Rory," Alana said, her voice low. She kept her eyes straight ahead, not looking at him.

"Aye, Bluebell?"

"I thank ye for showing me what 'tis like to be loved. I will cherish our time together fore'er."

He didn't think his heart could be crushed any further, but her words proved it could be. He scrubbed his hands roughly over his face, trying to clear the emotions that flooded over him. "I love ye, Bluebell. Remember that. Dinnae e'er forget it. My heart is yers. Now and fore'er. I only wish circumstances were different."

She nodded solemnly. "As do I." She swiped at the tears falling down her cheeks.

A MacDonell servant greeted them at the gate, and then rushed off to fetch her betrothed, Alana assumed.

"Thank ye," Alana whispered, as she glanced up at him, her eyes searching his, pain reflected in both of their gazes.

Not trusting himself to speak, he could only nod stiffly.

They remained silent until MacDonell arrived. Of course, as to be expected, the dolt was polished and poised, his arrogance wafting around him. He was the complete opposite to Alana's worn state. To her warm and caring demeanor. Michael MacDonell was shorter than Rory by at least a foot, but nearly twice as wide. The man's complexion was ruddy over blemished skin, and his hair was thinning at the top. One would never guess they were close in age.

How could he leave her here? He kept asking himself the same question over and over again. He had to bite the inside of his cheek to stop from pronouncing his love for her.

"Hart," MacDonell addressed him. "It took ye long enough. I expected ye here days ago." His voice dripped with aristocratic disdain. *Arse*, Rory thought. He barely glanced at Alana. He made no greeting or even an acknowledgment that she was standing there.

"Travel took us longer than we had originally anticipated. Weather and," he looked at Alana and pointed toward her ankle, "Alana hurt her ankle in a slip."

Finally, MacDonell's eyes slid o'er to Alana and with cold, gray eyes, he looked her over from head to toe. "I am to believe ye are weel now? I dinnae need to nurse ye to health, do I?" He snapped. "I do hope ye arenae the clumsy sort. I need a hearty wife, not a weakling."

Rory felt Alana stiffen against his arm. How he wanted to put his arm around her and tell her that all would be well. But kenning that would be a lie, he couldn't. And the show of affection would be of benefit to neither of them.

But Alana surprised him. She stepped forward, shoulders back, chin lifted, and addressed her betrothed. "I have recovered just fine. I am quite healthy as weel. Thank ye for yer concern," she retorted, and for good measure, she eyed him the same way he had her just moments afore, a bored look on her face.

If Rory wasn't so devastated of their inevitable parting, he would have broken out in laughter.

MacDonell wasn't as amused.

"My men arrived days ago with a claim that she had run off. But then a messenger arrived from Hartsmoor telling me that there was a carriage accident and she had been abandoned." He sniffed and regarded Alana again. "Those men that were escorting ye have been severely punished. They willnae be abandoning anyone or any of my orders again."

Alana gasped at the implication of what MacDonell had done to his men. Again, Rory wanted to reach out and comfort her.

MacDonell smacked the heels of his boots together, his hands clasped behind his back, and spoke to Alana. "Yer father assured me ye would arrive, and that ye were worth the price I've paid." His eyes leered over her body once again. "I am no' so certs."

Rory clenched his jaw to keep from retorting.

This wasn't his fight.

A servant appeared, different from the one that was waiting at the gate earlier. MacDonell regarded the young girl coolly. "This is Edna, yer maid. She will take ye to yer bedchamber." He turned his back to the woman and addressed Rory. "I assume ye and yer father are expecting compensation for escorting her here."

"Alana," Rory bit out.

"Excuse me?" MacDonell asked.

"Her name is Alana," he gritted out betwixt clenched teeth.

MacDonell waved his hand in the air in dismissal as if her name was insignificant.

Bloody bastard.

Realizing the women were still there, he turned back to them. "Why, pray tell, are ye still here?" He made a shooing motion with his hands acting as if they were animals. "Go, ye neednae stand here any longer."

Rory fisted his hands. It would be so damn easy to pound this bastard's face to a bloody pulp. And in the process start a clan war, he reminded himself, so he remained silent, watching as Alana followed Edna.

She glanced back—only once—but that one time was enough to twist the knife that had stabbed him in the heart even more.

"Weel, now that the women have finally left," he shook his head as if their presence was an inconvenience, "We can speak openly. Do tell, how is she? Other than easily injured?"

"I wouldnae say that is the case. 'Twas a bad fall."

MacDonell shrugged, not caring one wee bit for Alana's welfare. "I can only hope she's hearty enough to withstand our winters. She might be a good tup. I will find out soon enough. Hopefully, she's not barren."

Rory was speechless. Not because he had naught to say, nay, just the opposite. He was speechless because whatever he would say would surely have a negative impact on both Alana and his family. He didn't want to be the cause of her being harmed.

Oblivious to Rory's reaction, MacDonell continued. "Ye can

stay the night and sup since yer journey has been long, though much of that was yer fault. I expect ye gone in the morn afore I arise." He spun and headed toward the castle, not far behind Alana and her new maid.

Rory watched until Alana disappeared into the darkness of Caer Rannoch. It seemed to swallow her up and he could only hope that somehow, some way, she had the strength to find happiness in the life ahead of her.

As he made his way to the servants quarters, he could only mutter, "'Tis done." But it didn't feel like it.

$$\begin{array}{c} \longleftrightarrow \quad \bullet \quad \longleftrightarrow \end{array}$$

CHAPTER TWENTY-SIX

ALANA FOLLOWED EDNA into the entrance of Caer Rannoch and shivered at the sudden chill in the air. It felt colder inside than it had outside. She rubbed her hands against her arms to try to warm up.

Edna regarded her and nodded. "Yer trunks were dropped off earlier and brought up to yer bedchamber. We can go there now so ye can change into something warmer. Then I will show ye around the castle." They quickly moved through the Great Hall and Alana barely had time to look around. What she did see was that it was dark. Everything was dark here. The walls, the wood, the stone. It was cold, depressing. So unlike the home she had left behind. She would wager that Hartsmoor, Rory's home, was warm and inviting. The very opposite of Caer Rannoch. None of the lush greenery of the Highlands they had trekked to get here was present within these walls. A landscape that she had learned to love once she saw it through Rory's eyes and experienced it herself.

She followed Edna up three flights of curving steps, the stones so narrow that she had to place her feet sideways to climb them. She couldn't imagine how they delivered her trunks to her chamber up these narrow passageways. There was nay room.

On the fourth floor, Edna turned left. "Yer chambers are this way. Laird MacDonell's are to the right." She pointed in the other direction as if Alana didn't ken her directions.

At a set of double doors, Edna paused. "My laird gave no instructions other than to deliver yer trunks. If there is aught that ye need, please do tell, and I will do my best to see to it." She pushed open the doors and stepped aside for Alana to enter.

Surprisingly, the room was larger than the chamber she'd had at Auchenford. There was a large window covered with a dark blue tapestry with the MacDonell coat of arms weaved into it. A massive hearth offered warmth, or it would once the fire was built up. Across from the hearth, was a four-poster bed that held two pillows, a plaid in the MacDonell colors, and a throw folded neatly at the foot. A thick embroidered canopy was pushed back and tied to the wall on each side.

"Now that ye have arrived, I will have someone start the fire so ye dinnae get a chill when we return here." Edna took in her dress, muddy and dirty from their travels and clucked her tongue.

Normally, Alana would be mortified to present herself in such a matter, but not today. Each patch of dirt, each smear of mud, was a reminder of a moment with Rory.

Rory.

She closed her eyes at the pain that suddenly speared though her. Would she ever see him again? She didn't believe so.

Edna rummaged through Alana's trunks and pulled out a thick, green woolen dress, wool hose, a thicker shift, and clean boots.

"Let us get ye undressed and into this." She held up the clothes in her arms and then placed them on the bed.

"I could use a bath, methinks."

Edna tsked. "My laird doesnae care for such things other than for himself, but I am for certs that he will accommodate ye for yers. But he hasnae given permission for such a luxury yet, so I cannae fulfill yer request. Mayhap this eve after ye have had a chance to speak with him." She pushed Alana into a chair and began to tug her mud-caked boots off.

She hid the disgust she felt at having to acquire permission to bathe. What kind of man denied such a request? Apparently, the kind that she was to marry. For the umpteenth time, she tried to understand what her father had been thinking in making this arrangement, finally realizing that he had only been thinking of himself.

An hour later, Alana was seated at a long dining table across from her betrothed, a filled chalice of honeyed mead in her hands. Edna had done her best to clean Alana up and make her as presentable as possible, but the man across from her did not look happy.

She assessed him and determined that it should be she who was the unhappy one. The man was not old, but he looked old. Rory had mentioned they were close in age. She could not see that, and if she had met the man under different circumstances, she would have assumed he were closer to her father's age. Short and stout, with a round belly that affirmed he had never missed a meal. His balding pate was accentuated by the three long strands of hair he combed over to the side, trying, and failing, to hide the fact that he was, indeed, balding. His pockmarked skin was red and pale both at the same time. He didn't look healthy. He looked gluttonous.

He was a completely different visage than Rory. She would indeed be thinking of him oft whilst she was in the company of this man that would soon be her husband. Alana did all she could to control the shudder that overtook her at the thought.

"Is there a reason why ye have come to me dirty from yer travels?" he snarled, his lip curled in disgust.

"I-I thought I needed yer permission to bathe, my laird."

He scoffed. "Aye, weel, permission granted. As soon as we finish this conversation I expect ye to bathe. In the future, dinnae disgrace me with yer filth."

Alana only nodded. She didn't ken the circumstances regarding Edna and she would not say aught to get the girl in trouble.

"And ye will address me properly. Dinnae disrespect me with a nod." He pierced her with a glare until she understood his meaning.

"Aye, my laird."

"That is better. The wedding will take place in three weeks' time. The ceremony will be here. Yer parents may attend if they choose, but they are not needed." He spoke coldly, as if he were making a land deal. There was naught personal about his words. As a matter of fact, he had yet to ask her how she fared, or aught about her.

"Ye will see," he continued, "the Highlands are a much tougher climate than yer lowlands." He laughed. "I dinnae e'en ken why we bother with keeping the lowlands as part of Scotland. We might as weel offer the land to England. 'Tis the same thing."

"I dinnae believe that is the case at all. The land is quite lovely. Of course, 'tis no' nearly as mountainous as 'tis here, but it has 'tis own beauty."

MacDonell scoffed. "Spoken as someone who has only kenned that land. As I said, the King should order it be granted to England. 'Tis quaint with its flatlands and meadows."

Alana tried very hard not to feel affronted at the dismissive way he spoke of her home. But he was so cynical and dismissive that it was difficult.

"The Highlands build warriors. True warriors."

She couldn't fault him there, thinking of Rory. A definite true warrior. What was he doing now, she wondered. Scaling mountains that he couldn't when she was with him. Was he thinking of her as she was of him?

"Are ye listening?" MacDonell snapped.

Her gaze clashed with his angered one and he banged his fist on the table, causing her to jump.

"I apologize, my laird." She quickly tried to come up with an excuse for her not paying attention to his words. "I was only thinking of how lovely yer home is," she lied.

He regarded her for a moment, and then licking his thin lips, he smiled. "'Tis lovely is it no'? It has been in our family for generations and I dinnae see that changing anytime soon. We have a small chapel off the left wing. That is where our ceremony shall be held. Then we will have the bedding ceremony."

Bedding ceremony? Alana's heart jumped into her throat. Of course, he would expect to have a bedding ceremony. Lord help her. How? She did not ken how she could either get out of the bedding ceremony or manage to fool him into believing she was a virgin.

She smiled, but quickly stopped when he noticed.

"Aye, ye're looking forward to the bedding ceremony?" His eyes slid down to her bosom and then he leaned to the side, taking in the rest of her body. "It might be pleasurable—for me," he added with a chuckle.

Alana wanted to retch.

◆—————————————◆

CHAPTER TWENTY-SEVEN

RORY WAS PREPARING to leave Caer Rannoch and Alana behind. His heart as well. He was speaking with the stable boy regarding the supplies he would need for his return trip back to Hartsmoor when MacDonell came to find him.

"Ah, Hart, there ye are," he said. "I looked for ye in the Great Hall but must have missed ye," his sneer was condescending kenning damn well Rory had spent the night and meal with the servants and guards.

"Is Alana weel?" He asked, holding his breath when he realized what he had done—revealed too much.

MacDonell was smug when he answered. "She is fine. And she will forget ye soon enough. Dinnae fash o'er that. Once I have tamed her she'll be thinking of nay one else."

Rory stiffened, his rage flared as he fisted his hands. Yet, still, he managed to hold his tongue. But it took all his restraint.

"She seems to have developed a liking to ye. Have ye done the same? Do ye lust after my betrothed, Hart?"

"Nay," he lied through clenched teeth.

MacDonell shrugged. "It matters naught. Women need guidance, do they no'? She will learn."

Finally, Rory stepped in close to the man, looking down at him. "She is no' yers to tame," he growled.

MacDonell smiled then clucked his tongue, wagging a fat

finger in Rory's face. "Och, see, that is where ye are wrong, Hart. 'Tis the nature of things. Of bargains made. She may no' be mine this verra minute. But she will be. I will *make* her *mine*."

Rory's punch came without thought, connecting with Mac-Donell's beefy maw. The man's eyes widened afore he fell hard upon the bales of hay stacked near the wall.

Towering over the bastard, Rory seethed. "Ye willnae," he spat. "Alana would ne'er bow to ye."

MacDonell pushed himself up to stand. "I will," he countered. "If it takes me locking her in her chambers until she complies, she will obey me. I own her."

Rory's fist found MacDonell's jaw once again, and the man lilted on his feet, swaying for a moment afore catching his balance.

A few guards approached at the commotion, but they paused when Rory glared at them, blazing fury emanating off of him in palpable waves.

"Her father was a fool to strike a deal with a louse such as ye," he ground out.

"Mayhap, but a deal he did. A deal with the MacDonell," he jabbed a finger into his doughy chest. "No' with the Hart. Ye dinnae have enough to offer." He grabbed his crotch crassly thrusting his hips. "Ye cannae offer her this."

"Ye bastard!" Rory roared, rearing up to punch him again.

MacDonell put his hands up. "I wouldnae hit me again, Hart. I'll have ye in my dungeons so fast and no amount of sway will get ye released. I may e'en force ye to watch the bedding ceremony."

Kenning that he needed to get control of his emotions, Rory backed away. MacDonell was right. He'd punched him twice. The arse was a laird. He could already order him locked away. Nay, he needed to be smart.

He turned to leave, but paused, addressing MacDonell once more. "She deserves better. Ye ken it, though ye're selfish and dinnae care. I only wish she kenned it."

And then he left, his heart splintered into a thousand wee pieces.

◆━━━━◆ ◆━━━━◆

CHAPTER TWENTY-EIGHT

A LANA HAD JUST finished dressing and getting ready for the day when she overheard voices from outside. Angry voices. She rushed to the window to have a look and caught Rory punching her husband-to-be.

Nay! Alarm set in as confusion had her wondering what happened to bring the men to blows. Racing down the stone steps, she needed to get to Rory. She had to stop his assault. She had only been at Caer Rannoch for less than a full day and she had already realized how cruel and uncaring her betrothed was. She didn't want to think what would happen to Rory if he continued.

As she raced through the courtyard, closer to the men, the confrontation had already dissolved, and Rory was no longer in sight.

"Where is he?" She asked, her eyes darting around the landscape, trying to locate him.

"What does it matter? He is naught." He spit on the ground at her feet, and bloody spittle splashed on her boot.

The man was vile.

"What happened?" She insisted.

"Yer escort," MacDonell sneered, "insulted yer honor. I couldnae stand by and listen to such talk. I had to defend yer honor."

Alana didn't believe a word that he spoke. Rory would never

say such things. Even now, when his heart hurt for certs as much as hers. He wouldn't insult her. Nay, he had done everything to protect her. The exact opposite of what her betrothed had done.

"Ye are lying," she accused. "I demand ye tell me what truly happened."

He stalked toward her, grabbing her face roughly and forcing her to look at him.

She cried out at the biting pain his fingers caused.

"Ye dinnae order me aboot, bitch." He pushed her away from him and she nearly fell backward, laughing as he watched her. "Ye are mine now. What does it matter what really happened?"

Her gaze went to the trail that led to the gate and beyond to the lush Highlands, then back to the man she was supposed to marry, and everything clicked.

In that moment all of it came to light. The control. The disregard and disrespect for her as a person. The arrogance he held over her.

The future of what her life would be flashed in her mind's eye. She couldn't live like that.

Wouldn't live like that.

In a sudden burst of confidence, Alana took a step back, straightened her shoulders, and lifted her chin in defiance. Her voice was cold when she spoke. "Then ye dinnae ken me at all." In a swift move she ripped the engagement ring from her finger and hurled it at her betrothed's chest. "I would rather be free and ruined than married and controlled. Especially by the likes of someone as vile as ye."

MacDonell stood there shocked for a moment afore he gathered himself. "If ye believe ye leaving has any impact on me, ye are sorely mistaken. I didnae want ye anyhow. Who would? Ye for certs cannae bear me any bairns. Ye arenae hearty enough for that. 'Tis best ye leave now afore ye succumb to the blistery Highland autumn and winter." He moved to leave, but paused, tapping his finger against his temple. "Tell yer father I expect full repayment, along with interest for all I have had to deal with since ye darkened my doorstep with yer presence."

Alana only waited for a moment afore entering the stable and asking the lad there if Rory had left.

"Aye, my lady. Through the gate he went."

Biting her lip nervously, she kenned she wouldn't be able to catch him on foot. "May I have a horse? I promise ye will be compensated."

The boy thought for a moment. "I have just the one. He's mine, not the laird's and I've been training him. He's a good boy."

He disappeared out the back door of the stable and after a few minutes, returned with a beautiful chestnut horse and handed her the reins. He leaned in close. "Ye neednae repay me. 'Tis my gift to ye for escaping," he said with a wink. "Ye dinnae belong here." He helped her mount and then stepped back. "Travel safe, my lady," he said afore ducking back into the stable.

With a final look back at Caer Rannoch, she guided the horse to the open gate and kicked him into a trot. "Let us go find Rory!" She called, and only hoped she wasn't too late.

◆———————————◆

CHAPTER TWENTY-NINE

RORY WAS HALFWAY down the trail when he heard a horse galloping behind him, rapidly advancing. With his hand on the hilt of his sword, he jumped off the trail, turning to see who was approaching. He fully expected to see MacDonell's men, swords raised, ready to attack and strike him down.

Instead, his breath caught in his throat at the vision catching up to him.

Alana.

She was urging the horse forward, quick as it would go. She was breathless, her hair windswept, and the fiercest look on her bonny face. She would make any warrior a worthy opponent.

The horse skidded to a halt not far from him, and Alana dismounted, running to him. "I ended it," she said, her voice shaking, chest heaving.

Stunned, he didn't move as he absorbed her words. "Why?" He asked. "How? Ye had e'erything." But the words were bitter on his tongue. She didn't. He had left her in Hell and he kenned that.

Stepping closer, she shook her head. "I didnae. Without choice, I had naught."

He looked away, trying to understand what had happened. Was he dreaming?

He pinched himself and felt the smart on his skin. Nay, he

was wide awake and Alana was standing afore him.

His mind tried to assess what was unfolding. What the ramifications of it all would be. But, still, he had to ken the truth. To hear it from Alana's own lips. "Are ye for certs this isnae just yer rebellion talking?"

Reaching out, Alana grasped his hand, holding it betwixt hers and bringing it to her chest. "'Tis love talking. And if ye walk away, I will survive. Hardly, but I will. And I'll also ne'er forgive ye for it."

Still, he hesitated. Wondering if he should pinch himself again to wake him up because for certs this was a dream. Had he fallen and hit his head on a rock? Was his mind playing tricks on him? Mayhap the ale he drank at Caer Rannoch was poisoned in MacDonell's way of punishing him. Or the water he bathed in was tainted.

But then Alana cupped his face and brought his head down to her as she raised up on her toes, capturing his mouth in a fierce kiss that left no room for doubt.

Dropping his pack, he lifted her against him, wrapping his arms around her. Returning her kiss like he was starving for her touch. And he was.

When they broke apart, gasping for air, he stammered. "I didnae think I would e'er see ye again. The thought was killing me," he confessed.

"I couldnae lose ye, Rory." She stroked his cheek with her fingertips. "Walking away from ye last eve broke my heart. Spending any time with that, he is so vile I cannae e'en call him a man. I just couldnae. If my choice was to stay and marry him or throw myself o'er the cliffs, I would choose the cliffs."

"Dinnae think such thoughts, Bluebell. Ye are free."

She looked at him seriously. "I am no'."

He cocked his head to the side, confusion drawing his brows down. "Why do ye say that?"

A huge smile bloomed on her face. "Because I am yers."

He laughed, tumbling onto the ground with her, and pinning

her body under his. "Aye, but of yer own free will. I would ne'er tie ye down or attempt to control ye."

"I ken."

Their lips met once more. This time the kiss was slower, not as frenzied as afore, and Rory's body roared to life, his cock straining in his trews, weeping for release.

Rory lifted his head, looking around them. "Whilst, we appear to be alone, let us move off the main trail." He hopped up, and shifted his hard length to a more comfortable position whilst he collected his pack and grasped the horse's reins.

Leading them off the road, he played with the idea of getting her to the village, and renting a room at an inn for the night, but he didn't think he could wait that long to sink himself into her warm softness.

He located a spot that would offer them shelter in the chance of rain, and would hide them from any travelers. Tying the horse to a nearby tree, he opened his pack and laid out his blanket.

Afore he could say aught, Alana was there, stripping off her dress, sliding down her stockings after she'd kicked off her boots. Confidently, she stood there, in all her naked splendor, and crooked a finger at him, beckoning him closer. Moving quickly, he tore off his tunic. She didn't need to tell him twice.

They came together, fiercely, rushed. Worried that this could be the last time, but they both kenned it wasn't. There would be many nights ahead where Rory would take his time making sweet love to Alana. But not now. Nay. Right now, he needed to seat himself so far into her that he forgot his name as she writhed under him reminding him what it was.

Both naked as the day they were born, they fell onto the blanket. Rory's lips found Alana's pulse in her neck and nibbled, trailing small bites down to her breasts, where he pinched and licked and teased her nipples into hard peaks.

Beneath him, Alana moaned in pleasure, her fingertips feathering over his hair.

He dipped his fingers into her core, sinking into her wetness.

"Ye are so ready for me, Bluebell."

"I havenae stopped thinking aboot ye since yesterday," she whispered.

"I couldnae stop either."

"Make me yers, Rory Hart."

He smiled, and nudged her thighs open, entering her in one long, hard thrust.

Her breath caught on a gasp, and she smiled blissfully as she met his eyes.

Their coupling was swift, fast, and hard. As if they were trying to convince themselves that it was real. That they were truly together.

And when they tumbled over the edge together, calling out each other's names, Rory kenned that all would be well.

They slept for some time and when they woke, the sun was high in the sky.

Alana stretched, her beautiful breasts pointing to the sky above. Rory bent his head and captured a nipple in his mouth, tugging. She grasped his head and brought it up so she could kiss him deeply.

He sighed. He could spend all his days for the rest of his life and die a happy, sated man. But, they had business to attend. Things to discuss.

As much as it pained him, he stood, grabbing his trews and pulling them on.

"Must we leave?" Alana asked, her lips formed into a pout.

"Aye. There will be things we must take care of. First of which, the horse? Must we return it?"

She shook her head, her mussed hair swaying from side to side. "Nay. A gift from the stable boy."

Rory lifted a brow. "That was kind of him."

"I did offer him compensation, but he refused."

"And MacDonell? What of him?" Rory asked the questions that were burning in his chest. He wasn't sure where they went from here.

"He expects the coin he paid for me to be returned with interest for the inconvenience of dealing with me," she answered, rolling her eyes at the audacity of the bastard.

"He really is a louse."

"The biggest I have e'er had the displeasure of kenning."

Rory thought of her statement earlier. "Does yer father have the funds or has he already spent them?"

Alana sighed, shrugging her shoulders. "I dinnae have any idea, really. I hadnae realized how dour our financial situation was until I left. On our travels, I had a lot of time to reflect. I could see the signs. My father is inept at financial management. I see that now. He always comes up with some kind of scheme which nets him coin, and then once 'tis gone, he comes up with another one. I just happened to be his latest, and his last. Without me, he has naught left to bargain."

Rory pulled at the back of his neck. "So, the chances of him being able to repay MacDonell are unlikely."

"I believe so." She frowned. "What does that mean for us?"

He pulled her into his arms. "Dinnae fash aboot it. We will find a way."

And he would. He would take her to Hartsmoor and explain the situation to his father. Hell, if Moira could marry their enemy, then he for certs can take a wife that was originally promised to another. The Hart coffers were large enough. Rory would convince his da to repay the Duran's debt and then he would work to repay his father.

It might take some convincing, but he could do it.

He'd had Alana all to himself, then he had to let her go. Rory wouldn't make that mistake again.

SINCE THEY HAD the horse, traveling back to Hartsmoor went much quicker than their journey to Caer Rannoch. They did spend two nights at village inns. Rory smiled as he thought of the nights they spent learning every inch of each other's bodies. But more importantly, they talked. For hours on end.

He truly felt that he had met his soulmate.

"What are ye thinking aboot?" Alana asked.

"Why do ye ask? I am no'."

She twisted to face him. "Ye fib, Rory Hart. Yer arms tightened around me just then."

He smiled. "Cannae I just want to hug ye? But, aye, ye are right. I was thinking of us. How lucky I am. How ye came into my life at just the right time, and when I was least expecting it."

"I would argue that ye entered mine just in the nick of time. Saving me from a life of misery."

Now that the landscape had leveled out from the rocky terrain further north, Rory kicked the horse into a trot. "Ye dinnae give yerself enough credit, Bluebell. Ye would have saved yerself, I'm for certs of it."

She settled in front of him, her back to his chest, and he kissed the top of her head.

"Mayhap," she said quietly.

He nudged her. "Positively. I have nay doubt in my mind. Ye are the strongest woman I ken. No' many lassies would be able to face what ye had to and do it with her head held high."

"Do ye ken my parents are aware of what has happened?"

He sighed, maneuvering the horse around a large boulder. "They will soon enough. My parents as weel. 'Twill take a lot of explaining as to the e'ents of what have happened. But I believe we will win in the end."

"Getting away from MacDonell, I feel like I have already won."

Rory chuckled. "I can understand that."

"Really, I dinnae ken what my father was thinking." She huffed out an exasperated sigh. "Actually, I do. And I am no' happy to be part of his plan. He will have to find a way to continue Auchenford without bargaining off is family. Or, sad as 'twill be, Auchenford will fall."

"I am sorry, Love. I ken that is a hard realization."

She shrugged. "'Tis as 'tis meant to be. I love my parents, but I cannot continue to be controlled by them. And father will need to learn to depend on himself."

"Ye are a wise woman. Has anyone e'er told ye so?"

Alana laughed. "Nay, ye are the verra first."

The road split ahead of them, one way leading to the village that Rory had arrived at to escort Alana to Caer Rannoch, and the other leading to Hartsmoor.

Rory halted the horse, taking a deep breath. He was finally home. *Home.* He hadn't really ever felt that way at Hartsmoor. Only when he was hiking or scaling mountains did he feel at home.

But for the first time in years, he felt differently about the place he grew up. He wanted to show Alana Hartsmoor.

"Is something amiss?" Alana asked, looking at him over her shoulder.

Rory shook his head. "Nay. E'erything is as it should be." He dipped his head to the right. "Hartsmoor is just down that way. Are ye ready?"

She squeezed his forearms, and nodded. "I have ne'er been more ready for aught in my life." She turned and faced him. "We are in this together. You and I Rory. Together we can handle any situation."

He bent and kissed the tip of her nose. "I appreciate yer vote of confidence. I wish I could match it. I just want to start the conversations and settle e'erything. Only then, will I be able to feel the relief of kenning that our future together has been established."

RORY GOT A sense of deja vu as he entered the courtyard of

Hartsmoor Castle. Waiting for him, just the same as the last time he'd entered the courtyard, was his father, arms crossed, a stern expression knitting his brows together. Only this time, his older brother, Alpin stood beside his father, equally as formidable.

In front of him, Alana stiffened, and he heard her catch her breath.

"Dinnae fash, Bluebell. They are making a point, and 'tis directed at me."

He slowed the horse to a stop and dismounted. Turning to Alana, he lifted her off and onto the ground, ensuring that she was steady afore letting her go.

"Da, Alpin," Rory addressed the two men. "This is Alana Duran."

Immediately, Alana dropped into a low curtsy. "Laird Hart, Master Alpin. I am honored to meet ye."

Arthur Hart sighed. "Stand tall, Miss Alana. Ye neednae bow to me. Especially since it seems ye will soon be part of the family. I and my sons have much to discuss. I will bring ye to meet my—"

"They are here!" A shrill cry came from the bailey, and his three sisters ran outside, his mother close on their heels.

Rushing over to them, his youngest sister, Morven, arrived first, skidding to a halt, and smiling wide. "Ye are beautiful!" She exclaimed, causing Alana to blush. Rory couldn't help but notice how fetching she looked with pink tinging her cheeks.

"Morven!" Moira scolded, approaching them with a huge smile on her face. "Remember yer manners. Ye dinnae want to scare the poor girl afore she e'en has a chance to ken us. I am Moira."

"Och, she is fine," Alana said politely. "Thank ye for the welcome."

"And I'm Eilidh, the only level-headed one of the sisters."

Moira and Morven scoffed simultaneously.

"Alana. 'Tis lovely to meet ye, dear." His mother wrapped Alana in a warm hug. "Please ignore them. It appears I have raised heathens incapable of manners. I do hope my Rory has treated ye better."

Alana curtsied. "He was verra kind."

Lillias Hart gave her a warm smile. "I am glad to hear that." She lifted on her tiptoes and kissed Rory on the cheek, patting his chest. "She is bonny," she whispered in his ear. "Go with yer da. Explain yerself. He will understand eventually." She squeezed his hand and then turned to Alana, holding her hand out. "Come, let us leave the men to discuss matters no' of concern to us. Ye must be famished and exhausted. We shall get ye a hot meal and then an e'en hotter bath."

With a glance at Rory, she gave him a smile that made her eyes dance, and then allowed herself to be led away by his mother and sisters.

He watched until they disappeared inside and then turned his gaze to his father and brother, and now, Errol, Moira's husband who had joined them.

"Weel," his father started, "this was not the expected outcome I had anticipated when I tasked ye with this mission. But seeing the way yer eyes follow her e'ery move like a lovesick mutt, I would say we have much to discuss."

"Da, I—"

Arthur held a hand up, silencing him. "No' here." He turned and started toward the castle, the others following him inside and to his study.

Rory entered after his father, Alpin after him, and Errol last, shutting the door behind them.

At the sideboard, Arthur poured drams of whiskey and passed them out to everyone. He took a long swallow, nearly emptying the glass, and then refilled it afore sitting at his desk.

"The missive I received from MacDonell was no' a happy one."

"He was an arse to Alana. He—"

Arthur cut Rory off again. "I ken weel of MacDonell's countenance. The spoilt twit thinks too much of himself. Howe'er, rightly so, he feels wronged." He pierced Rory with serious eyes.

"Ye were there to deliver the man his wife, no' to fall in love with her and whisk her away."

"I did escort her there. I handed her to him. Kenning that was my duty. I fulfilled it."

Arthur raised a brow in question. "Ye delivered him a deflowered wife that was so besotted with ye that he could do naught with her."

Rory went to answer, but snapped his mouth shut. He couldn't deny the truth his father spoke.

"What is done is done. We cannae change that. Howe'er, MacDonell is threatening war unless he receives the restitution he has demanded. 'Tis a mighty sum."

Rory scrubbed at his face, realizing his beard needed a trim. The thought improper for the seriousness of the conversation happening currently.

Arthur looked at Errol, and then back to Rory. "I dinnae ken how I have managed to raise children that go against all the normal pathways of finding love." He regarded Alpin. "I can only hope ye and yer sisters will follow a more traditional path. First, I had to deal with the MacLeod for Moira, and now the MacDonell for Rory."

Alpin raised his hands in defense. "Dinnae look to me. I've no plans on marrying anytime soon."

"What of Effie?"

Alpin's face grew serious. "We are nay longer courting."

Rory frowned, wanting to ask what had happened, but Arthur cleared his throat, rapping his knuckles on the wooden desktop to draw their attention back to him.

"Back to the issue at hand. MacDonell is expecting a lot of coin for yer actions. The Duran's will be here in the next few days. Since they agreed to this match by promising Alana to MacDonell for a hefty sum, am I correct to believe they dinnae have the coffers to pay back what has been given?"

Rory gave a stiff nod of acknowledgment. "From the information I have been given by Alana, her father doesnae have a mind for handling finances. It sounds that he finds a new way to make a bargain e'ery few years. When the coin runs out, he thinks of something else. Alana was his final bargaining chip."

Arthur heaved a heavy sigh and leaned forward on his elbows, tenting his fingers under his chin.

"I apologize, Da. This wasnae aught I foresaw happening."

Arthur chuckled at that. "Ye forget yer mother and I were brought together by a mystical legend in a well." He smiled, easing the tension that Rory had been feeling. His shoulders relaxing a wee bit.

"What would ye like me to do? But dinnae ask me to send Alana back to her parents. I willnae. She will be my wife. Whether I have yer blessing, their blessing, or no'," he said fiercely.

"Ye love her?" Alpin asked, sounding shocked.

"Aye. With all my heart," he answered honestly, not caring if he sounded love swept.

For a long time, his father stared at him, until finally he spoke. "'Tis been a long time since I have seen ye passionate aboot aught but yer hiking. I will take care of MacDonell."

It felt as if a weight had been lifted off of Rory's shoulders. "Ye will?" He asked in surprise. Arthur nodded. "I will be fore'er in yer debt. I will repay ye, Da."

"We can discuss semantics later. For now, go bathe, ye stink of the road, and sup. Ye look like ye've lost weight."

Rory couldn't help the huge grin that broke out on his face. "Thank ye, Da." He bowed. "Thank ye." He rushed from the room, to bathe and sup as his father ordered, anxious to share the news with Alana.

CHAPTER THIRTY

THREE DAYS LATER, Alana stood in the courtyard of Hartsmoor Castle as her parents arrived. Their grim expressions made her aware to their real thoughts of all the events that had transpired since she had left Auchenford all those weeks ago.

Laird and Lady Hart greeted them and warmly welcomed them to their home. Her father shook hands stiffly with Rory's father and bowed to Lady Hart. Her mother curtsied them both. Both of their mouths set in a thin line.

Her nerves jumped as her parents approached Alana. She wasn't sure what she had expected their reactions to be. The time she had spent at Hartsmoor had been naught but cheerful. As Rory had warned, the castle was loud. His sisters made lots of noise. His brother and brother-in-law were raucous. And Alana loved every minute of it. It was so different than the quiet serenity of Auchenford. Not serenity, she realized now, but solemn.

She found that she preferred the noise over the silence. It brought a sense of happiness to her world.

Rory had told her about how the discussion with his father had gone. She was surprised at how accepting his father and mother were. She did not think her parents would feel the same. And from the looks on their grim faces, she was right in that thought.

Her father kissed her briskly on the cheek, and her mother did the same afore turning to Rory. Her father's eyes narrowed as he took the man she loved in, sizing him up to see if he was worthy of his daughter. She wondered why he hadn't put as much effort into finding that information out about Michael MacDonell. Her father had to crane his neck a bit to look in his eyes as Rory height was much taller than him.

"Rory Hart, I presume?" Her father asked.

"Aye, Laird Duran. 'Tis a pleasure to meet ye."

Her father harrumphed. "Mayhap if the circumstances were different I could say the same. Ye have placed us in quite the predicament."

Laird Hart cleared his throat. "Lillias, why dinnae ye bring the women to yer drawing room for tea?"

The lovely woman smiled, and she was lovely. Her fair hair and skin complimented her blue eyes. Whilst Rory favored his father's looks, he got his soft side, the one he kept hidden and unveiled only for her, he got from his mother.

Lady Hart clapped her hands together. "A lovely idea, dearest husband. Ladies, shall we?" She gestured toward the castle and Alana, her mother, and Moira moved inside.

As they walked, Moira hooked her arm in Alana's. She'd spent the last few days learning all about Rory's family, and she and Moira got on exceptionally well.

Inside, they moved to the second floor and settled into Lady Hart's drawing room, a comfortable and welcoming space that Alana had spent a lot of time in since her arrival. Overstuffed chairs were peppered throughout the room, offering ample seating. The hearth emitted plenty of heat to warm the room, and soon servants appeared with trays of tea and berry tarts.

At first, conversation was stilted, but Lady Hart had a way of making everyone feel at ease and conversation began to flow naturally.

Alana learned that her father had been angry when he found

out what had happened, but in the time since they first had received the news, he'd had time to contemplate the outcome. They had naught against Rory, and, when all was said and done, Alana learned that her parents were much happier that she had found love and solace with him and no' the MacDonell.

They did not discuss money as that was not their place and it was something that would be worked out betwixt the men.

By the time they had finished tea, her mother was smiling and acting much more of her usual self then when she had first arrived.

Later, when they were alone, walking the hall to the chamber that the Hart's had kindly granted to Alana, her mother paused, and pulled her in for a warm embrace. "I am happy ye found a man that looks upon ye as Rory does. 'Tis obvious he loves and cares for ye verra much, and ye him. Yer father will give his blessing. Dinnae fash out that. Or aboot us. We will be fine."

She hugged her mother back. "Thank ye."

THE DAY WAS sunny and warm when Alana and Rory exchanged their vows, promising to love each other throughout their days. The Hart chapel in which they had stood was quaint, but beautiful. Stained glass windows filtered the sun in colorful prisms that danced along the walls and floor.

Rory looked dashing in his formal wear, the Hart plaid secured over his shoulder.

Alana wore a gown of ivory layers that billowed like waves about her feet, which were encased in soft, silk slippers to match.

As Alana had appeared at the entrance of the chapel, her father at her side leading the way, her stomach did a flip at how handsome her soon-to-be husband looked. The huge smile on his face and the love and appreciation in his eyes nearly brought her to her knees.

But the kiss that sealed their union after they'd each spoken? Now that was worth a thousand lifetimes. Rory's lips had her toes curling and she couldn't wait for the celebration to end so they could retire to Rory's chambers.

Currently, her husband, och, how she loved the sound of that, was dancing a jig with Errol, and a dismal Alpin, who they had pulled onto the floor. The man had been miserable since his courtship with a lass named Effie had ended. Why he was so upset, she was unsure since he was the one to end it.

Beside her, Moira giggled at Errol's over-the-top movements. The love shining in her eyes was apparent to anyone that gazed upon her. She and her husband were very much in love. They defeated the odds that were against them. Much like she and Rory had done.

Eilidh, Moira's younger sister, played the fiddle with the other musicians, her fingers flying over the strings, and Alana watched with admiration.

"Eilidh is very talented on the fiddle," she commented to Moira and the woman nodded.

"Aye, she is. She actually travels with a band of musicians sometimes playing festivals and gatherings. Our da is no' a fan of her traveling, but her talent cannae be contained, so he allows it." Moira looked at Alana, her tone growing serious as she clasped their hands together. "I want to thank ye for showing Rory that he has worth. For a long time, he has been lost, unsure of his path. But no' anymore. Ye've brought the smile back on his face. It has been missing for quite some time."

"I could say the same to him for me. We found each other at the time when 'twas most needed—for both of us."

Errol and Rory joined them just then, out of breath and laughing. Alana handed Rory a chalice of ale and he drank deeply, her eyes drawing to his bobbing Adam's apple as she watched. She smiled. "Ye looked to be having fun out there." She nodded to the space where couples continued to dance.

He leaned over to kiss her cheek and whispered in her ear.

"No' as much fun as we will have later."

Her cheeks flushed profusely, and she looked around to see if anyone had heard, but the music and murmurs of the crowd were too loud.

Pulling her up from her chair, he led her into the middle of the room, Errol and Moira following closely on their heels. They danced for what seemed like hours afore she finally surrendered. "I cannae possibly dance anymore," she confessed, swiping her hair out of her face.

Rory leaned in close. "I believe we have made a proper appearance and can retire to our bedchamber for the night."

Her stomach did a little skip at the thought of the night ahead. It had been too long since she and Rory had lain together. She wouldn't disrespect his parents by doing so in their home without she and Rory being wed. He agreed and didn't pressure her. But she had expected naught less from him, though they did find plenty of alcoves to steal a kiss or two here and there.

Later, after they had stripped and freshened up, Alana lay back on Rory's huge bed and waited for him to join her. She didn't have to wait long.

"I have been looking forward to this night for what seems like fore'er," he said, lying down beside her, making the bed dip. He traced lazy circles over her bare stomach, then circled each nipple afore dipping his head down and catching each one betwixt his teeth, nipping gently, then licking away the wee bite of pain.

He kissed his way down her stomach, past her navel, and continued to trail kisses lower until he reached the apex of her thighs. He nudged them apart, baring herself to him and he grinned up at her. She was already wet for him. She'd been longing for this moment all day. Blowing on her damp curls, he tickled and teased, afore burying his face in her mons. His tongue darting out, licking up her folds, as she writhed and ground her hips under him. His tongue circled her bud of nerves, and then he sucked it into his mouth.

Her hips came off the bed, and a cry left her lips, her fingernails scraping along his scalp. "Rory!" She cried, and he chuckled against her, causing a whole new sensation that vibrated throughout her body. He continued until she felt as if she were going to go daft, and then he pushed a finger inside her, and she clenched around it tightly. Easing in and out, he added another, and then another.

Her breath came in pants, and she lost all control of her body. Unable to keep still, she writhed and bucked against him, and just when she thought she couldn't take any more, he brought himself up and captured her mouth in his. She could taste herself on his tongue as he plunged it into her mouth at the same time he thrust into her center.

"Oh!" She gasped, scoring her fingernails into his back. His pace was fast, quick, hard. They had been apart in this way for far too long. He plunged into her over and over. Deep as he could whilst he plundered her mouth.

Reality began to slip from her. She was going to go mad. She kenned it. She was feeling everything everywhere. That familiar feeling, that inferno that only Rory could ignite within her built. Grew, higher and higher, bigger, and bigger, as his thrusts grew more erratic, his breaths coming in her ear as gasps.

Then she was toppling over the cliff's edge. She'd climbed, and now she was falling. Fierce shudders overtaking her body and all movement was beyond her control, taken over by a passion so strong, it couldn't be contained.

With one strong, final thrust, Rory seated himself deeply inside her, spilling his seed, filling her, as he hollered out the pet name he'd given her. "Bluebell." The one she loved to hear him say.

A final shudder overcame him and he finally collapsed on to the bed on his back, drawing her with him so she lay atop him, nuzzling his neck, as he drew light circles over her skin, causing her to shiver.

"I fear ye will be the death of me, Bluebell," Rory said once he had gotten his breathing under control. "But I will die a happy man." He kissed the top of her head and pulled the throws over them.

"I dinnae want to think of yer death. We have many years ahead of us." She kissed his chest, the hairs tickling her nose.

"Aye, we do. I verra much look forward to what our future holds. As long as ye keep enchanting me, I will want for naught. I love ye, Bluebell."

She smiled into the muscles of his chest. "I love ye, too, Rory Hart. Thank ye for escorting me. In doing so, ye saved me."

"Och," he clucked his tongue. "Ye saved yerself. I was only there to support ye in any way that I could. Now, rest. 'Tis been a busy day."

It had, but it didn't stop them from waking up three more times during the night and showing each other how much they enjoyed their newfound freedom to come together whenever, and wherever, they wanted.

Currently, they were lying in front of the fire, the throws pulled off the bed and spread on the floor as Rory took his time loving her. She stroked his cheek, staring deep into his eyes, and wondered how she happened to get so lucky. The shadows of the flames danced across his face, making the dark flecks in his green eyes bright as he looked at her like she was his whole enchanting world.

It was the same way she saw him.

Sometimes one had to live through the bad to get to their happy ending.

They had done that. Allowing each of them to save themselves when it mattered most.

This man.

This man was her world.

Forever and always.

◄——————————————►

EPILOGUE

Three months later
Deep in the Scottish Highlands

ALANA STOOD IN a meadow that only weeks ago had been filled with the beautiful, vibrant colors of heather, staring at the modest cottage she and Rory built together. Well, she helped in any way she could, but he, along with the help of his father, brother, and brother-in-law, did all the hard work.

She wrapped the shawl she was wearing tighter around her shoulders, as a brisk wind moved past. The shawl was a gift from her mother-in-law. Lillias Hart was one of the sweetest people Alana had ever met. She very much stepped into the mother role and took over when Alana's mother made it kenned that she and Alana's father would nay longer be visiting. They were grateful for all the Hart's had done when it came to absolving them of their debts but found the situation embarrassing and Alana a reminder of the better days they were expecting. She tried to not let the realization that they were more concerned of their welfare than they were of hers drag her down to a dark space.

Instead, she held her head high, and bid them farewell.

Quickly, Lillias swept in, doing all the things a mother normally would for her child, and Alana hoped that she kenned how appreciative she was for that. For all of the Harts for that matter. They had all been welcoming and treated her as their own kin. It was a lovely feeling.

And now, as she looked at her quaint home, designed by both she and Rory, happiness overwhelmed her. They were still on Hart lands, but in a northern corner where no one else was about. Trees bordered the back of the house, the mountains close by, so Rory could hike and climb to his heart's delight. The meadow of heather surrounded them, and in front, they looked over a small loch.

It was beautiful, serene.

Quiet, calm.

"What are ye daydreaming aboot?" Rory asked from behind her, appearing with a fishing net slung over his shoulder, a huge smile plastered on his face. He lifted a bucket. "I caught supper." An even bigger grin transforming his face.

He bent and kissed her cheek, nodding toward her muddy hands. "Ye've been busy, aye?"

She laughed. "I wasnae daydreaming. I was admiring our home." She held her hands up, grimacing at how dirty they were. "I finished planting the herbs in the garden. I hope they can survive the winter."

"They will. I shall build a shelter around them to ensure they do."

"Ye are too good to me."

"Quite the contrary. I dinnae deserve ye." With a devastating smile, he disappeared inside the door, and she followed.

Moira and Errol joined them for supper. Out of all of Rory's siblings, Alana got on best with Moira. And though Rory and Errol got off to a rocky start when he first married Moira, Alana had watched their friendship grow and they now seemed more like brothers.

"We brought ye something," Moira said after they had finished eating the salmon that Rory had caught in the nearby river. She grabbed the bag she had traveled with and reached inside, pulling something to her chest, but Alana couldn't see what it was. "Now, first ye need to promise me that ye willnae laugh."

Alana was affronted. "Whye'er would I laugh at a gift given

from the heart?"

"Ye will see. Howe'er, I think 'tis important that ye ken that I am not entirely proficient in needlepoint."

Rory's eyes rounded. "Ye stitched?" He balked.

"Remember," Errol spoke up. "She stitched my wounds with adept hands."

Alana's eyes rounded. That was a story she hadn't been privy to.

Moira rolled her eyes. "Ignore them. Anyway, I made this for ye." She handed over a cloth and when Alana unrolled it, she sucked in her breath. Delicate stitching depicted their home, the loch in front, the mountains in the back.

"'Tis beautiful," she whispered.

"Dinnae look too closely. Ye will see otherwise," Moira jested.

"Nay. 'Tis truly a treasure we will cherish. Thank ye."

She stood up and wrapped Moira in a hug.

After stories of Rory's childhood and many teasing laughs, they said their goodbyes. Moira and Errol returned to their own home, even though Alana and Rory made the offer for them to stay for the night.

They waved their goodbyes and watched them disappear down the path and shut the door. Rory helped Alana with the dishes, and she was thankful for their unconventional partnership when it came to household responsibilities.

"I cannae remember a time when Moira picked up a needle and thread—that didnae involve stitching a wound—to create something to hang." He tilted his head to the side and studied the needlepoint that had been gifted to them. "'Tis really lovely. She really captured the beauty of our home and land. It must have taken her quite some time."

Alana wrapped her arms around Rory's waist and squeezed. "'Tis."

"On the morrow, I will make a frame to hang it in and then ye can let me ken where ye want it hung."

"That would be lovely." She lifted on her toes and kissed his cheek.

Later, as they sat in front of the fire, Alana rested her head on Rory's shoulder as they watched the flames dance.

"Do ye miss the life ye left?" Rory asked quietly.

She smiled and closed her eyes. "No' for a moment." She lifted her head and caught his gaze. "This," she waved her hand around their home. "This is e'erything I could have e'er wanted."

And she meant it. Could she have lived a life where she never wanted for aught? Where she had the money for whatever she wanted. She could have, but she would have been miserable. Life with MacDonell would have been hell on earth. She kenned that the moment she met the vile man.

But here, her life was full. She had everything she could ever want or need.

She had Rory. Her world. And soon, if her belief was correct, she would have a wee bairn. The first of many, she hoped. She had not told him yet. She wanted to be sure first. But she kenned how happy he would be at learning.

She brought her mouth to his, and he scooped her up in his arms, carrying her to their bedchamber.

Outside, the wind danced through the hills, and over the loch, chilling the air. But inside, there was only warmth—and love enchanted.

The End

About the Author

Award-winning author Brenna Ash is addicted to coffee, chocolate, and all things Scotland and BTS (the Korean band, not behind-the-scenes footage, though that can be fun, too!). She's a firm believer that one can never have too much purple or glitter. She loves rom-coms and always cries at the HEAs.

When she's not busy writing about Scottish Highlanders, Medieval Pirates, and Regency Rogues, she spends her time reading with her favorite music playing in the background, binge-watching Outlander, Bridgerton, and K-dramas, park-hopping with her daughter, spoiling her cats, Lilly and Mochi, or watching BTS content online. Brenna lives with her husband on the Space Coast in sunny Florida.

Website – www.brennaash.com
Amazon – amazon.com/stores/author/B01H46ZA02
Facebook – BrennaAshAuthor
Instagram – brennaashauthor
BookBub – bookbub.com/profile/brenna-ash